Rosamund and Sam look forward to living at the medieval manor house bought by their new step-father, Richard. But Richard soon takes a dislike to Sam and becomes over familiar with Rosamund. Her room is reputed to be haunted by another Rosamund, who lived there in Tudor times. As Rosamund faces an increasing threat of sexual abuse, it is the parallel struggle of the first Rosamund that helps her believe no one has the right to take over her body and mind.

THE GHOST PERSON

RUTH DOWLEY

THE GHOST PERSON

Andersen Press · London

First published in 2001 by
Andersen Press Limited,
20 Vauxhall Bridge Road, London SW1V 2SA

British Library Cataloguing in Publication Data available
ISBN 0 86264 338 4

Typeset by FiSH Books, London WC1
Printed and bound in Great Britain by the Guernsey Printing
Company Limited, Guernsey, Channel Islands

*To Judy and Anne
with love and gratitude for
many years of loyal friendship*

Looking Back

Rosamund and Sam rode their bikes from town. They turned in the gateway and saw Cleaves standing out against the woods, with its gables, tall chimneys and stone tower.

Half was still Richard's. For a fleet second, Rosamund panicked. The claw dug inside as it hadn't for months. She breathed from deep down there in her guts. In, out, in, out.

It's over. I'm looking after myself. I have help.

They pedalled to the southeast front and leaned the bikes against the wall of the enclosed garden. Rosamund looked up at the arched window of the room that had for a short time been hers – the room where embarrassment had turned to fear and fear exploded into terror, but also, thank God, the room that had belonged to the ghost person...

Chapter 1

'Keep quiet about it. What a jolly stupid waste,' Richard had said to Rosamund's mum after they heard the stories about the room. The last owners shut it up. They never went inside.

'I wouldn't want her to be frightened,' said Cathy uncertainly.

'You don't believe those absurd tales!' teased Richard.

He was so confident. What a relief to have someone to get rid of silly anxieties. Cathy laughed. 'Of course not. You're right. It would make a glorious bedroom.'

The school summer holiday started. Cathy and Richard came back from honeymoon and Rosamund and Sam from Aunt Susie's. The next day everything would be moved from Victoria Road. The manor would be home.

Could it be home, Rosamund wondered, when they drove up to the amazing house. Once before, Mum had brought them to look from the lane, but today the manor was waiting for them. Today they had a key.

'It's a mansion!' she gasped.

'Richard's only bought half, don't forget,' said Mum. 'Cleaves is built round a little courtyard.' But even half was a dream compared to their terraced house in the town.

'Impress-*ive*!' said Sam. 'SR goes for it, doesn't he?'

SR stood for Swanky Riches, a name Sam had given Richard behind his back the first time he arrived to fetch Mum in his Porsche.

'Stop calling him that. I told you,' Mum said, but not too crossly. She didn't want anything to spoil the visit.

'And he's not that rich. He has to work hard in his business the same as I do.' Mum ran the employment agency that their dad had started seven years ago.

'Bit of a difference in the readies though, huh?' said Sam. They stopped by a door studded with huge square iron nails. 'This place is ancient!'

'The tower's all that's left from the thirteenth century. The manor's been pulled about and added to ever since. A lot in Tudor times.'

'I bet there's a secret passage. Are the woods ours too?'

'No, but there's a right of way along the side by the stream.'

Mum turned the key and pushed open the heavy door. The summer's day disappeared. Cold met them as they stepped into a gatehouse set right into the manor building. It had flagstones and looked a bit like a church porch.

They stood for a moment in sudden absolute silence. It reminded Rosamund of holding your breath when you're afraid something is going to happen, but you don't know what. With a little shock, she recognised the feeling. It was how she often felt when Richard was around.

3

They went through a doorway on the right. A staircase rose out of a hallway, its elaborate balusters cut in dark wood. The stairs creaked and clacked under them as loudly as if they'd been on horseback.

'Is this the Tudor burglar alarm?' said Sam.

He leaped in front, taking the stairs two at a time, and flung open a door at the top. 'Swish! Who's in here then? You, Mum?'

She nodded. It was incredibly posh compared to Victoria Road with its own bathroom, a lush carpet and tasselled pelmets left from the last people. Sam whistled.

Mum laughed, all excited, and led them along a passage. Beams with woodworm holes showed in the walls between sections of plaster. Rosamund spotted the winding steps to the tower at the end.

But before they got there, Mum opened a door and announced, 'And *this* is Rosamund's room.'

Light streamed through an enormous high window of three arches in a stone frame. Under the middle arch, bits of coloured glass – red, blue, gold, green – were set among clear leaded panes like pieces of jigsaw spread for sorting. Their abstract shapes gave an uncanny feel of the present as well as the past to the ancient space.

'Oh, yeah! You're on the vibe in here.' Sam ran his fingers over the ridges on the oak panelling that covered two walls. Then he shot off to investigate the tower.

'There's a mirror already fixed, and plenty of light for your painting,' Mum said.

4

Rosamund looked around the room in disbelief. 'Is this really going to be mine? Did Richard say?'

'It was his idea,' said Mum. 'Well, we both thought you'd like it.'

Rosamund never imagined she'd be given anywhere so magnificent. 'I adore it!'

'Do you?' Mum suddenly turned and hugged her as if she were relieved. Rosamund nestled into her shoulder.

It seemed a long time since they'd hugged. It felt like Mum was trying to make up for spending so much time with Richard. Perhaps by giving her this beautiful room, she was trying to say everything was going to be good now.

Mum kissed her cheek before letting go. 'We'll get you some new curtains,' she promised. 'Nothing from Victoria Road will fit here.'

Sam burst back in. 'There's a room up there! Can I have it, Mum? It's awesome!'

'Just a minute, darling,' said Mum, considering the window.

Rosamund thought how pretty she looked, even with her hair pinned up at the back. She wore it like that when she was doing messy jobs or when she had on her 'serious' suit for important business meetings.

'What do you think?' she asked Rosamund. 'A cotton print?'

'I'd like flowers,' said Rosamund.

Beside himself with impatience, Sam grabbed her sleeve. 'Pick the flowers later! Come and see the *tower*!'

'Unhand me, sir!' said Rosamund, mimicking a Tudor lady. She looked down her nose. Sam was three years younger, shorter and thin and wiry.

He stuck out his tongue, then grinned.

The wedged-shaped slabs winding up to the tower room dipped in the middle from hundreds of years of treading. The way was so narrow you could touch the wall on one side and help yourself up on the central stone column on the other.

At the top, windows looked out in three directions. An alcove cut into the thick wall on the northeast side. Standing in the alcove, you could see for miles, past the woods, over fields to the church and the ruins.

The other way, you saw past Rosamund's big window and into a garden belonging to the other part of the house. It lay below, a bright square divided by little paths.

'Look at the garden,' Rosamund exclaimed. 'It's like an embroidered cushion.'

'Exquisite!' agreed Mum.

Over the far wall of the garden you could see the gateway into the grounds.

'This has got to be my room!' shouted Sam, dashing from one lookout point to another. 'Blast! Look, these iron rungs must have been where you climbed up to get on the roof. Some idiot's plastered the ceiling over!'

'Thank goodness for that,' said Mum. 'I expect it was unsafe.'

'Can I have this as my room? Can I? Oh, *please*, Mum!'

'No, you rascal. We couldn't get your bed up those stairs.'

'I'll sleep on the floor. Think how good it'll be for my back.'

Rosamund saw Mum hesitate. She wanted to please Sam. 'We'll see what Richard says,' she told him.

'SR'll let me if I suck up to him.'

'Stop talking like that! You must both remember he's in the family now.'

Rosamund didn't like remembering, but the thought of her wonderful new room made her feel better.

Sam looked towards the gateway. 'Who's the old dear with the fruit and nut cake on her head?'

A woman walked to the walled garden with even steady steps, carrying a basket over her arm. She wore an elaborately decorated straw hat.

She glanced up at the faces in the tower. She smiled and waved. The three of them waved back.

'That must be the widow who lives in the other half,' said Mum. 'She owned all of Cleaves once. Aunt Susie likes her a lot. They raised money for Save the Children together. Now – to work! I've got to be changed and at the agency by twelve.'

They were going to get the kitchen ready for tomorrow. They'd brought basic things for the first day.

They carried boxes along the ground floor passage, past echoey rooms. The big sitting room had a mantelpiece carved with leaves and plaited corn.

Sam disappeared, cleaning rag in hand, while water

heated in the kettle. After a period of quiet, they heard him exclaim, 'Hello!'

Mum called, 'Sam, you're skiving.' She wrung out her cloth in soapy water.

A moment later, he slipped into the kitchen and sidled up beside them.

'Surpri-ise!' he sang.

Rosamund and Mum jumped. Something live danced on the platform of his open palm. He held its slender tail between the thumb and finger of the other hand.

'Good grief!' cried Mum. 'What's that?'

'A little mouse.'

'Crumbs!'

'Yeah, thanks. He'd like some.'

'Put it outside!'

'I'm keeping him. He's going to be my mascot.'

'Darling, no.'

'How did you catch him?' asked Rosamund.

'He came out in the passage. I dropped the cloth over.'

'Can't you get a better hold?'

'You shouldn't pick up mice round their bodies. They hate being squeezed. Will had one once.'

The tiny creature had bright black eyes and ears like delicate brown sea shells. Its pointed face was fringed with whiskers.

'He's sweet,' said Rosamund. 'If he doesn't bite.'

'He's not going to bite. It's a young one. He's friendly.' Sam thrust out his hand. 'Look, Mum.'

Mum backed away, her rubber gloves dripping wet splodges on the tiles. 'I don't need to see any closer.'

'He can live in the tower with me. I'm calling him Homer, because I found him in our new home.' He gave Mum his impish grin.

Rosamund giggled. It was an obvious get-round, but a hard one for Mum to resist.

'I'm going to find something to keep him in.'

Sam turned on a trainer heel and evaporated again into the silence of the house. Mum let him.

Rosamund didn't mind. It was fun doing things just with Mum. Before Richard, they used to cook together sometimes. They'd have the radio on, and the windows of the kitchen at Victoria Road would get steamed up. They used to experiment, adding stuff the recipes didn't say.

It had been a shock when Mum said she was going to marry Richard, but she'd been so excited about how marvellous it was going to be for them all. Rosamund liked her being happy. She knew it had been difficult working and looking after them since Dad died.

If only Richard didn't make her feel uncomfortable. She kept noticing him watching her. And he made comments about how attractive she looked, touching what she was wearing as he admired it.

She hoped she'd get used to him. Her friend Julie's parents were divorced. Now Julie's mother was married to Rob, and Julie really liked him.

They wiped inside the drawers and cupboards, and

scrubbed the work surfaces. When they set out coffee mugs for the moving men, Mum said, 'Better put the biscuit packet in that plastic container in case Homer has any friends.'

Rosamund glanced at her. They burst out laughing. They often laughed about Sam when Mum gave up on him.

He showed up again right on schedule when all the jobs were done. He started hunting through junk left behind in the storeroom off the kitchen.

Mum's mobile rang about some agency problem.

Rosamund went back up to her room. She decided she would put her bed against the panelling with its head under one side of the arched window. She would put her easel the other side, by the wall with the mirror.

The sun came out. It shone through the maze of leaded glass on to the mirror.

The mirror tilted slightly on the uneven wall. The coloured glass was reflected onto the panelling, especially in the corner opposite the door. The moving branches of a magnolia that grew outside the window made the colours appear and disappear.

I could paint that, she thought.

The big door must be open downstairs. She could hear a breeze coming in. It wisped about the room, making a gentle sound like a voice asking, 'Who? Whoooo?'

She smiled. 'Rosamund,' she answered in a whisper.

The little wind sighed, 'Ahhhh.'

Chapter 2

The moving van from Richard's place blocked the drive in front of the gatehouse when they arrived late next morning.

'There you are! Jolly good.' Richard strode out buoyantly and grabbed Mum. He kissed her on the lips even though he'd seen her a few hours ago at Victoria Road.

She almost disappeared as he wrapped round her. Richard had played rugby when he was younger, but now the large body below his broad shoulders was more fat than muscle. Bulge without the baby, Sam called it.

A couple of sweating men edged past with a polished table.

'My desk. In the library,' Richard told them, releasing Mum. 'First room off the hallway.'

'How do you like Cleaves?' he asked Rosamund and Sam. He sounded sure of their answers.

'Brilliant!' said Sam.

'And what about miss?' He put his arm around Rosamund as if they were mates.

'It's beautiful,' she said. She eased away shyly.

He gave an approving nod. 'Isn't it super!' He turned to Mum. 'I've almost got this lot sorted out. These chaps should be finished before the van from Victoria Road gets here.'

'Excellent organisation as always,' said Mum, beaming at him.

The moving men arrived at the hall door with his desk. 'I say, I don't think you'll get through that way,' he called into the gatehouse. 'Tilt it!'

'We can do without a scratch,' he said to Mum. 'That's a valuable piece.' He frowned and shouted, 'Try tilting it!'

The movers staggered on as they were. The desk passed through undamaged.

'They were jolly lucky!' Richard said.

Rosamund hoped the men didn't hear. Richard strode after them. They all followed into the old library, listening as he gave orders about the position of the desk.

'More to the middle, please. No, *this* way.'

'Yes, sir!' Sam mouthed at Rosamund with a grin.

'I thought your desk could go by the fireplace, Catherine,' said Richard.

Sam swivelled his eyes. Everyone else called Mum 'Cathy'. He squatted to examine a load of electronic equipment on the floor.

'Better leave that, Sam,' Richard boomed across the room. 'I'll show it to you later.'

'Want me to help you set up the PC? Are you on the net?' asked Sam. 'Looks like a spare line over there we could use for your fax and answer phone.'

'He's used to all this gear from the agency office,' Mum said.

'Jolly kind of you, Sam, but I've got another job you

12

can help with this afternoon.' Richard gave Mum a confiding smile. 'I don't think we need junior aides in here. It'll be a real nerve centre when we merge.' He wanted Mum to join the agency with his company.

Mum laughed. 'Now we've been through all that. Advice, I'm grateful for, but no take-overs!' She smiled up at him winningly. 'This is certainly going to make a splendid place to work at home though! I hope I can keep a cool head amid such grandeur.'

Richard rumpled Mum's hair, looking pleased. Rosamund felt conscious that this was his house. Nothing was really theirs, even though he was their stepfather.

She realised that she hadn't had the word stepfather in her mind before. Nothing seemed fatherlike about Richard.

Father. Daddy. She didn't remember him as a picture, although of course they had photos, but as a kind of safe presence. Holding on to his hand with both of hers and leaning back while he talked to someone. Going to sleep snuggled against him on the sofa at Aunt Susie's.

'Excuse me, love,' said Richard, brushing against her as he went past to direct the moving men. 'My bedroom,' he called. 'First at the top of the stairs.'

'*Our* bedroom,' said Mum, laughing again.

'Absolutely,' agreed Richard. He clamped her in a full lock for another kiss as the men heaved a chest of drawers up the rackety staircase.

Sam raised his eyebrows at Rosamund. He gestured

outside with his head.

They went through the gatehouse and started walking around the manor.

'Poor old house. Bet it itches,' said Sam. He pointed at the grey and yellow lichen mottling the stones. They looked like scabs.

Rosamund smiled. She felt glad Sam was there.

They headed towards the tower in the east corner. The ground dropped about half a metre on the northeast side. Sam jumped down, ducked his head and did over-arm strokes along the wall.

'I'm in the moat!'

'Do you suppose that's what that was?' asked Rosamund.

'Bound to be. Much deeper of course. We did moated manors at school. Basic fortification.'

This part of the grounds was rather neglected. A lot of bushes grew near the tower base.

On the southeast side, they walked under Rosamund's window and up to the gate into next door's walled garden. Sam nudged Rosamund.

'The fruit cake's being aired again,' he whispered.

Rosamund saw the decorated straw hat down among the flowers.

'Sh!' she giggled.

The hat moved and the old woman raised her head.

'Is it my new neighbours? Come in,' she called cheerfully. She stood up with the help of the garden fork stuck in the earth beside her.

The garden glowed like a wonderful room. Roses and vines wove through trellises against the walls. In front of them were seats covered in grass.

'Your garden's even more beautiful down here than from the tower,' Rosamund said.

'Thank you, dear. I've tried to make a garden like Cleaves might have had in its early days.'

'Nifty cutting up the square shape with these little hedges,' said Sam.

'Pick something from them.'

They bent and pinched off wispy silver-grey fronds from the shrub edging the path where they stood.

Rosamund sniffed. 'Is it a herb?'

'Cotton lavender.'

Sam darted to break a piece from another border. 'What's this spiky job?' He raised the sprig to his nose and inhaled with exaggeration.

'Most healthful.'

The old woman laughed. 'That's rosemary. There are a lot of herbs here. You can imagine how welcome their taste was before refrigerators when food was apt to go off – and their scent with only primitive waste disposal. Not to mention the need for medicines. But what are your names, my dears? I'm Lucille.'

'I'm Sam.'

'I'm Rosamund.'

'Rosamund?' Lucille repeated wonderingly. Her eyes went to the house. 'A lovely name. An old name. Well, well.'

15

As she looked upwards along the manor, towards Rosamund's room in fact, the sun reached under the hat and shone on her face. The skin had a million tiny creases like fragile tissue paper. Her hair was so white as to leave not one strand to tell what other colour it had ever been.

'Did you know that a woman called Rosamund lived at Cleaves in the sixteenth century?' she asked.

'Really?' exclaimed Rosamund.

'Perhaps you're her reincarnation, Ros,' chaffed Sam.

'She's buried in the church down near the ruins. She was born in 1509, the year Henry VIII became king.'

'Do you know anything about her?'

'I know... a little. I have something of hers. Why don't you both come to tea on Wednesday, if it's all right with your mother, and I'll show you?'

'I'm afraid I'm going ice-skating for my friend's birthday,' said Sam.

'Then perhaps you'll come, Rosamund, and Sam will come another day?'

Rosamund felt easy straight away with Lucille. 'I'd like to. Thanks.'

It was weird thinking of someone with her name walking about here almost five hundred years ago.

Lucille led them to the middle of the garden. An extraordinary rosebush grew where the paths met. The flowers were *striped* – deep crimson over blush pink.

She cupped a hand gently under one of the blooms. 'This rose is called Rosa mundi.'

'Gosh!' said Rosamund. 'Wow.'

'Listen.' Sam tore to the gate. 'It's our furniture van!'

'Off you go then, dear,' called Lucille, laughing.

Sam shouted, 'Thanks. 'Bye! See you!' The gate clanged behind him.

Lucille picked a stripy flower and offered it to Rosamund. She smiled kindly. 'Will you take your rose?'

The centre of the flower glowed with gold. Rosamund accepted it, a little awed.

'Oh, thank you!' It seemed a special present.

Knowing about the other long ago Rosamund felt like a present too.

Before opening the gate, she looked back and saw Lucille still standing in the middle of the bright garden. Rosamund was certain she was thinking about the coincidence of the names.

As soon as her things started appearing out of the van, Rosamund went up to her room to unpack.

A deep stone ledge ran at shoulder height along the bottom of the high window. She arranged her jewellery box and hairbrush on the mirror wall side, her paints in the middle and a row of her best books on the side over her bed.

She carefully cleaned and filled one of her painting jars in the bathroom that had been made in the tower on that floor. She stood the Rosa mundi rose in the water. It rested its round face on the rim of the jar and glowed up at her.

17

She set the jar on the ledge under the arched window beside her books. A soft gust of air ruffled the rose petals.

She looked along the window for a draught gap. Although she felt the edges of all the lower panes, she couldn't find one.

Sam's things were directed to the room originally planned for him, but from the constant scuffling past her door, Rosamund guessed that he was quietly shifting them. A gargantuan grunt eventually made her come out and have a look.

A mattress stuck out of the bottom of the tower.

'Sam?'

His voice came down the spiral. 'Give that end a push, will you?'

They bent the mattress from top and bottom and urged it round and round up the stone steps. They laid it out behind the door and collapsed, panting.

'Have you asked Richard if this is okay?' asked Rosamund.

'It'll be too much bother to say no after I've moved everything.'

'I hope you're right.'

Across the room near the alcove, she saw a cupboard with a wire mesh door. 'Is that Homer? Where did you get the cage?'

'It's an old food safe. It was lying about in that storeroom off the kitchen.'

The wooden shelf had broken. Sam had made half of

it into a ramp, creating a spacious two-storey house.

Homer was evidently burrowed out of sight among shredded newspaper in a private upside-down box bedroom. A heavy bowl filled with water and a snack of muesli and bits of carrot waited at the ready on the ground floor.

'Do you think it's cruel keeping him shut up?'

'He'll only be in there when I'm busy. He'll soon be tame as anything.'

Mum called up the big staircase. They ran along the passage and looked down. She stood flushed on the bottom step, her hand clutching the carved finial at the end of the dark handrail.

'All right?' she asked eagerly.

They nodded.

'Richard's going to order some pizzas. What kind would you like?'

'Cheese and mushroom, please,' said Rosamund.

'And peppers,' added Sam.

'We'll ask what they've got. Your bedding's in that box there just outside our room. You could make your beds.'

'Okay,' said Sam. 'We'll do it now.' He grinned at Rosamund.

'First time in history you've been in a hurry to make a bed,' she said as they dug out their things.

They groped back down the passage with duvets and pillows balanced from arms to foreheads. Sam staggered on up to the tower.

'See you later!'

Rosamund turned into her room. Something swished like a curtain or a full skirt. She tried to peer round the bedding. The corner of her eye caught a flicker of vapoury light, and, at the same moment, she thought she heard a faint exclamation of greeting.

She dumped the pile and looked about. No one was in the room.

Chapter 3

Don't start imagining things, Rosamund told herself.
Old houses have all sorts of quirks that take a while to
understand.

It was reassuring to remake the same bed she'd slept
in last night at Victoria Road. She smoothed the bottom
sheet and settled her pillow in place. Her nightie went
under the duvet. A soft rabbit Mum and Dad gave her
when she was little went on top.

When she'd finished, she picked up her hairbrush and
wandered over to the mirror. Her hair was getting really
long. It came halfway down her back. She didn't have a
fringe, so it often fell in her eyes.

She stopped brushing and gathered the hair. She lifted
it to see how it would look put up like Mum's. Not that
good. Dreamily, she let go. The hair fell in sections
which crossed over one another, giving her the idea of
plaits.

Her fingers separated the front hair on one side of her
central parting into three strands. They wove together
into a flat plait so easily that it gave her an odd feeling.
It was almost as if someone expert were helping.

She got a fastener from her jewellery box. Then she
did the other side with the same strange sense that she
was being taught.

The two plaits made a decorative band around her

head when she scooped them together over the long loose hair at the back. She tucked them into each other and fixed them with grips. She turned to the side. It looked fabulous.

Sam poked his head into the room.

'Knock, will you?' said Rosamund. 'I might have been changing.'

'Pardon me, my lady.' He doffed some imaginary headgear with an elaborate courtly gesture. 'Mum wants you to lay the table.'

'What are you doing?'

'Holding SR's bottle racks while he screws them in place. I'm being *jolly helpful*,' he added, imitating Richard's voice.

Rosamund thought of saying *Super*! back in the same voice, but she found it hard to joke about Richard.

Anyway, he couldn't help his over-the-top way of talking. It was how he was brought up. And it didn't sound as if he'd had that great a childhood. He hadn't asked his parents to the wedding. He said he never saw them now.

Richard and Sam were working in the cool whitewashed storeroom off the kitchen where Sam had found the food safe. It was in the base of the tower and had no windows.

Richard was going to cover the whole wall opposite the door with wine racks. 'Make a jolly impressive display when I open up,' he told Sam.

Mum was on the phone to the agency, energetically

22

sorting out the latest problem. She covered the mouthpiece when Rosamund came in. 'Do the table, will you, darling?'

When she rang off, she added, 'Two lots of glasses. Richard's got some champagne.' She was on a high. She tipped out a bag of salad. 'I like the plaits! You've done them beautifully.'

A bowl of flowers had appeared on the kitchen table.

'Where are these from?' Rosamund leaned down and breathed in the scent. For once her hair didn't fall in her eyes.

'Lucille next door brought them. Aunt Susie's right – she's a treasure.'

'She gave me a rose. It's got my name.' Before Rosamund could tell her any more, Richard and Sam came in from the storeroom.

'Look at Rosamund's new hairstyle,' Mum chirped.

'Mu-um!' The last thing Rosamund wanted was to have Richard stare at her.

He stopped and looked immediately. 'Jolly attractive. Definitely the manorial miss!' His eyes followed her round the table as she put down plates.

'Don't be silly,' Rosamund mumbled. She felt herself blushing.

'She's the Lady Rosamund,' said Sam.

'Shut up, Sam!' Rosamund stuck out her head and wrinkled her nose at him.

'Oh, *un*ladylike!' said Sam.

'Didn't they use to chop off the tongues of

disrespectful women?' Richard teased.

'They tied them to stools and dunked them in the river,' said Sam.

'No horror stories, please,' Mum cried, laughing. 'Let's have the champagne.'

Richard brought the bottle to the table. 'Dom Perignon, '85!' he announced.

'Is it going to explode?' asked Sam. 'Can I catch the cork?'

'This isn't Asti Spumante, young man! Watch me. You hold the cork and turn the bottom of the bottle.' He gave a smooth twist and the cork jumped out with an obedient phut. 'There! Nothing wasted.'

He carefully poured into four glasses and topped up three. He gave full ones to Mum and Rosamund and the not so full one to Sam. Sam flicked his eyes between his and Rosamund's glasses, putting on a wide exaggerated smile. Rosamund held in a giggle.

Richard stood at the head of the table. 'This is a jolly satisfying moment. I've always wanted a place like this. You're going to make a smashing hostess, Catherine. Here's to life at Cleaves!'

'And to happy families,' said Mum. She and Richard touched glasses.

Then they clinked with Sam and Rosamund. Richard smiled knowingly at Rosamund as their glasses touched. He seemed to insinuate some understanding between them. She felt confused.

Sam took a gulp and got bubbles up his nose. He

started coughing. 'Too much fizz. Uh!'

Mum rubbed his back. 'Don't swig it like lemonade!'

The pizzas arrived and filled the kitchen with their delicious crusty smell. Richard put a bottle of red wine on the table for after the champagne.

He tickled Rosamund's waist as he passed. 'Need any help with your room? I could give you a hand later.'

'No, thanks,' she said, startled by the sudden contact.

'Oh, such a serious miss!' exclaimed Richard.

Mum glanced up in a way that showed she thought Rosamund was being unfriendly.

Sam joined Richard in helping himself to a selection of pizza.

'You must know a lot about wine,' he said conversationally.

'I think I can say I do.'

'Have you got a lot of special stuff in there?' Sam gestured with his head at the stack of unpacked cases in the new wine-store.

'That wine's worth a lot of money. I've got a lock to put on the door, Catherine.'

Sam gave Rosamund a quick amused look that said, Does he think we're going to nick his booze or something?

While they ate, Richard described his buying expeditions to wine caves, pronounced the French way to rhyme with halves. Sam nodded with interest as he worked through the pizzas. Not that Richard wasn't keeping up. He had a colossal appetite. There wasn't

25

going to be any difficulty finishing all of the four extra-large he'd ordered.

'Now this wine,' said Richard, pouring himself a second glass of red, 'I got at a bin-end auction. It's got an unusual nose.'

'Snooty, is it?' inquired Sam.

Richard laughed. 'You're a wit. Nose refers to the smell of the wine. Anyway, I spotted that the catalogue had the wrong vintage. Nabbed two cases for a real knock-down.'

'Devious!' affirmed Sam.

Richard sipped contentedly.

Sam turned to Mum. 'By the way, I've moved my things up to the tower myself so's not to cause any trouble.'

'You scamp! I said we had to ask Richard about that first.' Mum smiled at Richard. 'Sorry – I told you about his rascally scheme! ' She looked back at Sam. 'Richard wants to use the tower.'

'Yes, sorry, old chap,' said Richard. 'It's perfect pre-dinner entertainment. Take people up with a drink to survey the domain.'

'Oh, I won't mind your friends coming up,' said Sam agreeably.

Rosamund saw Mum waiting to see if Richard would relent. Mum was caught between them.

'I expect your friends would think you were really kind if you let Sam have the tower,' Rosamund said. 'They'd understand what fun it would be for him.'

Richard gave a roar of a laugh. 'They would, would they? I see the manorial miss is going to be exerting feminine wiles to get round the lord.'

Rosamund felt herself blush again. She wished she hadn't said anything.

Richard went on watching her. 'So you think little brother should have it, do you?'

'Tweet little brother,' Sam twittered, putting his head on one side like a cute Walt Disney waif, making the whole thing ten times worse.

Rosamund stared at her plate.

'And Mother obviously does too,' taunted Richard. 'What a conspiracy! '

'No,' said Mum. 'I only said he could ask.'

Richard leaned back. 'How can I refuse my ladies anything tonight of all nights? They've won it for you, young man.'

Mum beamed.

'Brilliant! Thanks!' said Sam.

'You must have it neat as a barracks when we're entertaining mind.'

'Oh, *absolutely*.'

'And, Sam, there's no need to put pizza crusts in your pocket. There isn't going to be a famine at the manor.'

'They're for Homer. My mouse.'

'Mouse! I didn't know you had a white mouse.'

'He's not white.'

'What colour is it?'

'Sort of browny grey.'

'Sounds like vermin.' Richard roared with laughter again.

Rosamund realised that Richard probably wouldn't approve of Homer.

Mum seemed to get the same message. She jumped up. 'Now who would like some fruit to finish?'

'White mice are the same as house mice,' persisted Sam. 'They're just albinos.'

'Would you like an orange, Sam?' asked Mum, fixing him with a warning look.

'No, thanks. I'll have one later.'

'Richard?' said Mum, offering the fruit bowl. 'You two can be excused when you're finished. There's not much clearing up tonight.'

'Right! Thanks for the pizzas and champagne and everything.' Sam scraped back from the table and scooted out.

He'd pulled it off! Rosamund tried to catch Mum's eye, but she was fussing round Richard.

She wandered out of the kitchen and into the big sitting room, weaving through boxes waiting to be unpacked. She was glad to meet some familiar things, but it was strange having them mixed up with Richard's stuff.

Their finger-marked music centre squatted uneasily on his polished side table. His stiff chairs ganged up round their comfy sofa. The chairs seemed so tightly stuffed beneath their expensive fabric that no one could ever sit comfortably on them.

In fact, all his furniture could have come straight out of a shop. She supposed that was because he was divorced and didn't have children. There hadn't been anyone to mess it up.

Her stomach felt tense when she went to bed. Everything was so different from Victoria Road.

She wanted to go and find Mum, but Richard might be in the bedroom. Richard would always be around now. She decided it was that, more than moving, which bothered her.

When she switched off her bedside lamp, moonlight came through the uncurtained window and traced the outlines of arches and window panes across the room. The great house became utterly still.

Then faintly, very faintly, Rosamund thought she heard singing. Could it be coming from next door? Women singing. Soothing voices, rising and falling in a sweet simple melody.

She suddenly felt tired. She curled up and went to sleep.

Chapter 4

Sam spread forgotten friends on the floor round him as if he were opening Christmas presents. They were unpacking boxes in the big sitting room.

Richard stepped over games, comics and sports gear with increasing irritation as he went back and forth to sip the wine he had resting on the ornate mantelpiece.

Sam tipped out the music tapes.

'Hey, I didn't know we had this one!' He slapped a tape into the deck in the music centre. Hectic dance music rollicked through the sedate room.

'Turn that racket off!' Richard shouted.

'Oh, don't you like it?' asked Sam innocently. 'Lucky the tower's out of the way. I'll play it up there.'

'Yes, take it away, and any other object in which you have an interest. We're supposed to be creating order in here, not getting ready for a car boot sale!'

Mum delved into a carton. She pulled out a large print. 'Yours, Rosamund.'

Richard moved to have a look, taking the hint that they needed a distraction. 'Bit of a self-satisfied woman.'

'It's a self-portrait by Gwen John,' said Rosamund.

'I *see*. A woman artist. I'll carry it up and hang it for you.'

'I can take it,' said Rosamund. She grabbed the picture. 'I don't want it put up till I decide the best place.'

She started out of the sitting room. Mum frowned at her.

'Thanks though,' she added, embarrassed. She hadn't meant to be rude. She just didn't want Richard in her room.

Sam followed her with the box of tapes.

'Come straight back for the rest of your mess,' Richard called after him.

'Yes, Sir Richard,' Sam quipped when they were out of earshot. 'That's what SR is going to stand for here. Let it out last night, didn't he? Thinks he's a lord now he's got a manor.'

'Half a manor,' corrected Rosamund.

Sam chuckled.

With no curtains in their rooms, Rosamund and Sam woke early at Cleaves. Rosamund went up to the tower first thing on Monday. She liked seeing Homer have his breakfast.

She watched entranced as the little mouse picked up oat flakes one at a time and sat back on his haunches. He held them like a sandwich, taking tiny rapid bites.

When he'd finished eating, he cleaned his face and behind his ears with his paws like a cat. Then he picked up his tail and worked on cleaning that.

'Oh, Mum. Look how sweet he is!' Rosamund exclaimed when Mum came to find them before going to work.

'Hmm,' said Mum without committing herself. 'I'm

off now. You two are going to be all right, aren't you? You've got the agency number and the mobile, and there's Lucille in an emergency.'

'We'll be fine, Mum,' Rosamund said.

'We're not babies!' said Sam.

'Of course, you're not, darling.' She gave them both a hug instead of the usual quick kiss.

Rosamund was looking forward to today. Julie was coming out. She could show her Cleaves without Richard there.

Julie was more than impressed. 'You jammy Joe! This place is *so* cool.'

After inspecting house and grounds, they lounged on the bed in Rosamund's room.

'You have to remember it's not ours though,' said Rosamund. 'It's Richard's.'

'But it's the same. He's like your dad now. I wish Rob were a rich businessman, instead of a teacher. No, that's a lousy thing to say.' She put her hands together and intoned, 'Forgive me, Rob.' She laughed. 'I like old Rob the way he is.'

'Did you always like him? From the beginning, when your mum started going out with him?'

'Not like I do now. I mean, I get mad at him when he and Mum close ranks and won't let me stay out late or something, but Dad would be the same. Did Richard buy you the easel?'

'It's a present for him and Mum getting married.'

'Brilliant.'

'He gave Sam a penknife with gadgets.'

'What's wrong with that?'

'It wasn't nearly as expensive.'

'Don't you want the easel?'

'Of course. I've always wanted one, only it seemed unfair. I felt awkward.' Rosamund looked at the paper she had stretched on her drawing board the day before.

'I know. Stand down there by the panels, and I'll sketch you. That corner is magic when the sun comes out.'

'Okay.' Julie sauntered down the room, swinging her hips. 'I suppose famous beauties have to submit to being ogled.'

'Why?' Rosamund pulled her chair to the easel and sat down.

'Why what?'

'Why should someone be stared at if she doesn't want to be, whatever she looks like?' She shut one eye and held her pencil at arm's length to measure Julie's size in proportion to the panelling.

'Because she won't be able to stop people. Boys, men, that is!' Julie giggled. 'Mind you make me worth ogling!'

As Rosamund squinted across the room, she seemed to be looking through a brown wash. Julie became blurred. She looked as if she were wearing a long dress.

Rosamund's outstretched arm suddenly went tingly. She lowered it. She tried to put down the pencil, but it stuck. She shook her hand. The pencil fell to the floor.

33

'What's up?' asked Julie.

Rosamund wiggled her fingers and rubbed herself. 'My arm's gone to sleep or something.'

Julie came over and massaged into the muscles. 'Okay now?'

'Yeah. Thanks. Anyway, it gave me the idea of painting you to match the room. In Tudor clothes.'

'Romantic!' Julie went back to her pose.

'It wasn't romantic if you were one of Henry VIII's wives and had your head lopped off,' said Rosamund.

'That's true!'

Rosamund remembered pictures she'd seen of the wives. She picked up her pencil and sketched a figure in a tight bodice with a square neck. The sleeves tapered at the wrist and the skirt was full. The edge of the paper rustled as she drew.

'They had head-dresses in those days, didn't they? Probably needed them. There's a funny draught in this room.'

'Is there? I can't feel anything,' said Julie. 'Oh, I wish I could stay the night!'

But she couldn't. Her family was leaving for two weeks in Devon next morning. Rob came to fetch her.

'Ask me over the minute we're back,' she called to Rosamund out of the car window.

'Promise!' Rosamund called back.

Rob smiled and waved in an matter-of-fact ordinary way. You could imagine him as part of your family.

*

That evening, Rosamund decided she'd paint Julie's face and the Tudor clothes, and then, if it were sunny in the morning, she'd do the coloured lights on the panels.

She went to fill her jars in the tower bathroom. She gave a start as Richard came out. She thought he would always use the bathroom in his and Mum's bedroom.

'I'm j-just getting some water for my paint brushes,' she stammered.

'Super. What are you painting? Let me see.'

'I haven't done anything yet.'

He stood and watched while she filled the jars. 'Will you paint something for me?'

'Oh, I'm not good enough,' she mumbled.

He shot out a hand and tickled her waist. 'Your pictures are smashing.'

A jar slopped over into the sink. She refilled it.

'I told Catherine we should put one up in the kitchen,' he went on.

Mum had framed a few of her paintings. At Victoria Road, they'd been in the living room.

Richard followed her down the passage with a hand on her back. She focused on the water level in the jars, finding it difficult to hold them steady.

'Let's see how your bedroom's turned out,' he said, coming straight in. 'Oh, jolly nice! I knew it was too good a room to waste.'

Was that a compliment? Did he mean he thought

she'd know how to appreciate the room properly? Well, she did like it. She ought to show she felt grateful.

'Thank you for letting me have it instead of making it a guest room or something,' she said shyly.

'And you're using the easel.'

He seemed to want to be thanked again for that too.

'Yes, it's good.' That didn't sound enough. 'It's great being able to support the painting and shift back to the right angle. You know, low for water colours so they don't run...'

He wandered over to the bed and touched the duvet with his fingertips. Her nightdress poked out at the top. Her rabbit looked childish. His hand drifted up and rested on its leg.

For some reason, it reminded her of the day he'd taken the whole family to the Grand National. When Mum went to the loo before the race, Richard had asked Rosamund about school. He was sitting next to her in the grandstand. He put his hand on her knee. She had wished he'd take it away, but she'd been too polite to move.

Now she fiddled with the paintbox. It was dreadful having him scrutinise everything. She couldn't think what else to say.

'Anything you need for in here?' he asked.

'No, thanks. I've got everything from home.'

For a moment, his expression was disappointed, pleading even. 'Tell me if there is.'

He wants me to like him, thought Rosamund. I

should try to be friendly. 'I really think this room's terrific,' she said.

'Super!' He was confident again. He smiled at her in that knowing way she didn't understand.

She pretended to wash a brush. She wished she could vanish.

He stood watching another few seconds and then walked slowly out. He touched her hair as he passed.

She tiptoed after him and shut the door. She felt jittery. Perhaps he would be satisfied now he'd seen how she had arranged things. If he didn't use the tower bathroom, he had no need to come down this end of the passage.

She mixed a golden-red in one of the dips in her paint box lid. She wanted to make a rich-looking gown.

The draught breathed through the room again, cooling her flushed face.

She decided to put on a little of the background to firm the line of the body before she started the dress. She rinsed her brush and mixed yellow ochre with a touch of black. The uneasy memory of Richard in the room stayed at the bottom of her mind as she worked round her Tudor girl. She added a little more black and a little more.

The edge of the paper trembled. Her sketch of the panelling began to disappear as she worked on in a trance of concentration.

Suddenly, she blinked and stared at the picture. A ghostly white figure stood out from horrible muddy

37

darkness. She dropped her brush in the jar.

Honestly! What possessed her to use all that black? She'd never be able to put on the coloured lights now. She'd have to start all over again!

The picture was spoilt.

Chapter 5

Rosamund watched Mum flick through the papers in her briefcase before going to work Wednesday morning. Richard had just left.

Sam scurried in for his lift into town.

'You and Will come straight round to the agency after the skating,' Mum told him. Will was coming back to spend the night.

'Oh, moan! We'll be hanging about ages while you just finish something.'

'I'll do my best not to be late, but things come up.' She sounded harassed.

'Why don't you chuck working so hard now you're married to SR?' said Sam.

Mum's lips straightened to a tight line. 'Don't you start! The agency's kept me going since Dad died. I'm not giving up running it!'

Sam grinned. 'That's the stuff, Mum. Don't cave under to Sir.' He pronounced cave like the French wine places.

'Don't talk like that! I want our new family to work as well. You could make more of an effort towards it by being tidy. You annoy Richard unnecessarily, leaving things all over the place. And, Ros, you could try to be more sociable. He says you close up every time he tries to get to know you better.'

39

'I'm sorry,' said Rosamund. 'He makes me feel embarrassed. Putting his arm round me and tickling me and stuff.'

'He's trying to be warm. He may not get it quite right, because he's not used to children. He's thrilled about having a daughter.'

'Not keen on ready-made sons?' inquired Sam.

'Stop it, Sam!' Mum warned. She snapped the briefcase together and blew Rosamund a kiss. ''Bye now, darling.' She hurried off.

Sam grinned at Rosamund and shook a finger before racing out to the car.

That afternoon Rosamund did her hair carefully in the new style and went round to Lucille's. A little table stood ready, pulled up to one of the grass seats.

'They're turf benches, dear,' said Lucille. 'They were used from medieval times. But I do like a plump cushion on top.' She patted the one she'd put for Rosamund.

China cups and plates with a pattern of flowers were arranged on an embroidered cloth. Lucille had made cucumber sandwiches so thin that they really did melt in the mouth. There was bread covered in honey, walnuts and banana rounds, and a crumbly rich cherry cake.

'You've been to so much trouble just for me!' said Rosamund.

'For my new friend, I hope.'

The scent of honeysuckle wafted from a trellis behind the turf bench. Nearby, birds hopped in and out of a birdbath. They ran about the paths radiating from the Rosa mundi rose as if they felt completely safe in this enclosed garden.

When Lucille cut the cake, Rosamund couldn't resist a glance at the straw hat. There were no nuts on it, but plenty of cherries and flowers.

'You're noticing my funny old hat,' Lucille said. 'I decorated it myself years ago. I cut the flowers from scraps of silk.' She laughed good-naturedly. 'I got carried away rather, but it's cheerful.'

Rosamund laughed with her. 'Sam thinks it looks good enough to eat!'

After tea, Lucille took Rosamund inside her part of Cleaves. They turned from a passage straight into a large room with wooden rafters holding up the roof. The perfume of the garden came with them, living here in bowls of potpourri.

'This was the great hall of the manor house,' Lucille said. 'Not as large as halls were in medieval times. Rosamund's father made a lot of changes in the early sixteenth century and a smaller hall was one of them. Still too big for me to heat in winter though. I retreat to my snug sitting room at the end of the screens passage.'

She pointed through the panelling crossing the end of the hall where they'd come in. Above it was a wooden balcony.

On another wall hung what looked like an immense canvas joined together in strips. Someone had painted it with scenes, but they were faded and the material was ragged in places. On the right-hand side, a big hole gaped.

'There you are, dear,' said Lucille. 'The story of the first Rosamund of Cleaves, if you can read it.'

'Who made it?'

'Rosamund had it painted. It's recorded in an inventory. Painted cloths were popular wall coverings. They were cheaper than tapestries.'

'And it's still here, after all this time!'

'Cleaves only left descendants of Rosamund's family in the nineteenth century. Then it wasn't lived in for thirty years until my parents restored it in 1928. Nobody bothered to take this away. Dirt and damp and rats had done a fair amount of damage by then.'

'Is that Cleaves in the top corner? There's the tower! Is that a moat? Sam guessed that dip on our side was left from one.'

'Good detective. There was a moat round Cleaves until the eighteenth century. The stream was diverted to feed and clean it.'

'And there was a bridge.'

'Two bridges. One by your front door which belonged to the gatehouse and more of a service one this side built by Rosamund's father near the hall. Can you see Rosamund?'

A slender figure with a long skirt stood by the house.

'Oh, yes!' Although the head wasn't clear, she seemed young, only a few years older than Rosamund herself.

'She's holding some flowers.'

'If you look carefully you can see there are flowers all around her,' said Lucille.

'Yes! Flowers and little animals.'

'Those flowers started me making the garden. It's pure fancy, but I imagine Rosamund loving flowers.'

In the scene, trees grew to the side of the manor. Among them lurked a dark figure, painted like a shadow, perhaps meant to be hiding. The figure gave Rosamund an uncomfortable shivery feeling.

'Who's that man?'

'My guess is that it's her cousin. We know from letters that he arrived with some retainers soon after her father died, supposedly to help her sort things out. Actually, he was scheming to get hold of the estate. Moved in and more or less took control. He tried to force her to marry him.'

'Did she marry him?'

'There's your answer, dear. Along here.' She pointed to a group of buildings inside a wall. A nun had an arm around a bending Rosamund.

'What's happening?'

'She's seeking refuge in the local convent. The ruins of it are down by the church.'

'What happened to Cleaves?'

'The cousin lived in it for a time, but Rosamund was safe.'

'And in the end?'

'Letters were written. Pressure was put on the cousin

to leave. Much later on, Rosamund married someone of her own choosing.'

'My father died too,' said Rosamund, then wondered why she had. Perhaps she wanted Lucille to know Richard wasn't her father.

Lucille nodded sympathetically. 'I remember how it hurt when my father died.'

Rosamund considered the idea of an old woman once having a father who died. Everyone loses her father sometime, she thought.

'Would you like to go up on the minstrels' gallery?' Lucille asked. She pointed at the balcony.

She took her back into the passage behind the wooden screen and up some stairs.

They passed the entrance to Lucille's bedroom at the top and walked along the gallery where musicians had played for long-ago feasters below. The panelling at the back seemed familiar. Rosamund touched the carving.

'That's linenfold panelling, cut to look like pleated cloth,' said Lucille.

'It's the same as in my room.'

Lucille turned quickly. 'Why, which is your room?'

'The one by the bottom of the tower steps. '

'Then it's on the other side here.' Lucille paused for a moment. She searched Rosamund's face. 'Are you liking Cleaves, dear?'

'I think the manor's lovely, yes.'

Lucille smiled. 'I'm glad,' she said.

With a hand against the panels, she paused again. Her

gentle eyes rested on Rosamund's hair. 'I hope you'll come to see me often.'

Rosamund felt that there had been something she decided not to say.

Chapter 6

When she was in the kitchen next morning, Rosamund heard metal grating against stone. She carefully pushed open one of the windows. It had a pretty lattice of diamond-shaped panes.

Rasping and thudding came from near the tower. The bushes shook.

Rosamund went out and ran along the moat dip. She saw their wheelbarrow from Victoria Road standing a little way from the end.

She peered through the branches. Sam had a spade and Will a garden trowel. They were digging like demons.

'What are you doing?'

'Historical research,' said Sam without pausing. 'Don't tell anyone though.'

'What do you think you're going to dig up?'

'It's better you don't know. Then the inquisition can't make you talk.'

Will sniggered. He uncovered a stone and lobbed it over the bushes.

Sam pushed out, balancing a spade-load of earth. He tipped it on the mound already filling the wheelbarrow and bumped off towards the woods.

Rosamund saw she wouldn't get anything out of them while they were hyped up. She went back into the manor.

She had prepared a new piece of paper, done a sketch, and was ready to have another go at the Tudor girl.

In her window, glass jewels glowed in sunshine. The coloured lights flitted about the oak panelling as the tips of the magnolia branches swayed outside.

Today the air inside the room was calm and scented. She and Lucille had picked lavender from one of the little hedge borders. She had tucked it in the side of the mirror to dry.

Rosamund felt content as she painted. No one would interrupt. She began to have such a sure sense of how the figure should be that she might have been painting from life. The certainty took over from any idea of making her like Julie, though she had a warm feeling while she worked as if she were painting a good friend.

The girl looked wonderful in her rich gown. She faced Rosamund joyfully. It seemed as if she might spin off the paper laughing. Round her danced all the colours of the artist's palette, all the colours of Lucille's garden.

Rosamund hummed as she washed her brushes and emptied the water jars in the tower bathroom. Her room seemed to buzz with excitement when she returned. This was the best picture she'd ever done!

She hurried to the easel. As she turned, she glanced into the mirror. She was looking at the corner she'd been painting.

Someone stood there among the coloured lights. Someone smiling. She saw her through a bright haze which sparkled and dazzled. The happy feeling of

47

friendship she'd had while painting came again.

Then in a flick of light, in a fraction of a second, the person faded. She melted into a panel and was gone.

Rosamund spun round. Her ears rang as if she had been called. Except for the shimmering colours, the corner of the room was empty.

Had it been a trick of the light? She searched the mirror. Nothing.

Could her painting have got reflected somehow between the window glass and the mirror? She walked round to where it leaned on the easel.

She studied the lively face and the golden-red Tudor dress. Was that what she'd seen? Yes, something like that.

She put down the jars. She sat on the bed and picked up her rabbit.

Her eyes travelled to the opposite wall where she had propped the spoilt picture over her Gwen John. The blank figure outlined in darkness gaped back.

It certainly hadn't been like that. It hadn't been scary. It had been ... wonderful!

She pushed her nose and mouth into the softness of the rabbit. Her warm breath came back onto her face.

She had seen a ghost!

As the thought settled into her mind, she heard a distant shattering of glass. Sam and Will rushed in downstairs, shouting.

A stone from the archaeological dig had smashed through one of the kitchen windows. Four of the diamond-shaped panes were broken.

Richard was furious.

'This leaded glass is a nightmare to replace. Takes a specialised glazier. It was *asinine* to play ball that close to the manor!'

When Sam owned up to a 'throw' hitting the window, Richard assumed it had been a ball.

'I'm really sorry,' said Sam. 'I'll save up and pay for it.'

He sat at the kitchen table looking grubby enough to be a chimney sweep. Mum stood beside Richard, frowning.

Rosamund watched them anxiously. She blamed herself for not realising this might happen when she saw stones being unearthed.

'Catherine, I don't think he should have boys here while we're out,' fumed Richard. 'They tempt each other into mischief.'

He picked up the telephone and glared underneath at the directory and Mum's phone-number book. 'I'll have to track down a glazier by tomorrow. We've got Howard Hunt and the Crosbys coming for dinner on Saturday.'

'I don't suppose they'll see the kitchen,' Mum soothed.

'We're going to give them a tour. I want to show Crosby the wine. Where are the Yellow Pages?'

'In the library.'

Richard slammed down the phone. It dinged in protest. He stamped out.

'Who does he think he is, saying I can't have my

friends over?' said Sam. 'I can, can't I, Mum?'

'You've been very irresponsible.'

'It was an accident, Mum,' Rosamund said.

'Don't make excuses for him!'

'I've offered to pay,' railed Sam. 'He wants to boss everything. Sir Richardhead! He thinks he owns us.'

'Don't be rude! Can't you see how difficult you make it, doing things like this?' Mum hurried out. Her heels tapped quickly up the stone flags to the library.

'Imagine banning someone's friends because of an accident!' cried Sam.

'She'll talk him round,' said Rosamund.

'She's got her own problems with him. I heard them last night when I was fetching me and Homer an apple. He was putting on the pressure.'

'What about?'

'Stitching up the agency. And he's giving other people the impression she's going to let it happen.'

'How do you know?'

'I check his answer phone.'

Rosamund and Sam had supper by themselves. In spite of the tense atmosphere, Rosamund badly wanted to talk to Mum.

She wanted to tell her about the ghost before she told Sam. She hoped Mum wouldn't think she imagined it.

She hung about, but Mum was in and out of the library doing agency things. In the end, Rosamund went to her room.

She didn't feel frightened in the room. But she did feel extra sensitive as if all her senses were on alert. When she was unplaiting her hair in front of the mirror and the door opened, she jumped a mile.

Richard stepped in. His anger seemed to be gone. He gave her that confusing knowing smile. 'There you are! No need to hide away. I don't blame you for your brother's stupid behaviour.'

He handed her a bag. 'Picked these up for you in town today.'

She felt herself blush as she took out some tubes of water colours.

'You shouldn't have. I've got paints.'

'The salesgirl said those are unusual colours.' He looked at the easel.

'I see you've been busy. Oh, *jolly good*! I definitely like you as the manorial miss.' He wrapped his arms around her from behind so that they could look at the picture together. She went rigid to show she didn't like it, but he didn't let go.

The draught stirred in the room.

'It's not me,' she said.

'It looks like you. Thought you were doing a self-portrait like that woman artist.'

'It's just someone I made up.' Rosamund tried to think how to release herself politely.

Richard gave a roar of laughter. 'And you're making up ghosts too!'

Rosamund started. 'What do you mean?' She felt the

breeze moving round them. It shivered against her skin.

Richard pointed at the spoilt painting on the floor, apparently finding it very funny. His arms leaned each side of her neck, pulling her back against him.

The breeze made a hissing sound, like a warning. Why couldn't he hear it? She felt desperate to get away.

'That painting went wrong,' she said.

Richard relaxed his arms and let them press intimately against her chest. Rosamund felt so embarrassed, she could hardly believe that it was happening. Didn't he realise what he was doing?

The hiss deafened her. In its midst, she thought, *he shouldn't touch me like this. I know he shouldn't.*

She ducked under his arms. She made for the door. 'Thanks for the paints. I have to go and ask Mum something.'

'She's on the phone to Aunt Susan.'

'Oh, good. I'd like to say hello.' Rosamund stumbled out into the passage and half ran to the top of the stairs.

She heard Richard following. Even now she wasn't going to be able to talk to Mum alone.

Chapter 7

The glazier came the next afternoon. Rosamund and Sam watched him fix the kitchen window.

The little panes had to be cut individually to shape and the lead remoulded over the edges. The man worked patiently, intent on doing a good job. Afterwards, he walked around the outside of the manor admiring the old windows.

'Now there's another one looks as if it had bit of a smash,' he said, standing back beneath Rosamund's room. 'And that's real old glass, that is. I reckon that glass went in with the window 'bout the sixteenth century.'

'Would all the odd shapes have been part of a design once?' Rosamund asked.

'Certain. Could have been a coat of arms or just decoration. Any painting on the colours?'

'I haven't noticed.'

'That could give you a clue what it was.'

Sam tilted his head at Rosamund. 'Got to be on the lookout for clues at Cleaves.'

Rosamund wrinkled her nose at him. He was still being infuriatingly secretive about what he'd been up to with Will.

'Glass was precious,' said the glazier. 'They would've picked up all that could be saved and soldered new lead

53

to reset it. That's why you've got that crazy-paving look where all the broken bits have been put back in.'

As soon as he tidied his tools into the travelling workshop in the back of his van and drove off, Rosamund raced up to her room. There *were* black lines painted on the coloured glass. She couldn't make any sense of them though.

She moved her books. Clinging to the side of the stone window frame, she climbed from her bed onto the ledge. That brought her level with several pieces of green and red.

Some of the painted lines were very fine. But she saw what they once created. She bounded down.

She ran to Lucille's and banged on the open door.

'Do you know about the glass in my room?' she called when Lucille appeared in the screens passage.

'No, what, dear?' asked Lucille, full of interest.

'We had a glazier here. He says it's from Rosamund's time. And it used to have *flowers* painted on it. If you get up close you can see parts of petals and leaves.'

'I was sure she loved them!' exclaimed Lucille. She came out into the garden beside Rosamund and looked about delightedly. 'Perhaps that glass was put in to please her.'

'Could it have been?' asked Rosamund. 'I don't suppose you know what the room was used for then?'

'Yes,' said Lucille, meeting her eyes. 'There are records of the changes Rosamund's father made in 1520 after his wife died. He loved his only child very much.

54

He had it panelled specially as a chamber for her to sit and sleep in.'

Rosamund stared at the bush of striped roses in the centre of the garden. So now she knew. The ghost she had seen was the first Rosamund of Cleaves.

On Saturday, you could hardly move in the kitchen for the heaps of food. Mum and Richard were making difficult recipes.

There was no comradely chucking things in with a hope and a giggle. Richard even reweighed some flour when he thought Mum was getting slapdash. Rosamund helped, but felt completely out of it.

'How about a little Muscadet?' asked Richard, taking some wine out of the fridge.

'Don't think we need a drink this early, do we?' said Mum.

'Why not?' He opened the bottle.

'Not for me, thank you,' Mum said crisply. Rosamund had seen her noticing how much Richard drank. Sometimes she put away a half-drunk bottle at the end of a meal, but Richard always had it out again.

He poured a glass, then turned his head and gave Rosamund a conspiratorial smile, 'Like some?'

'Of course she wouldn't, you ninny,' Mum said.

'Come round the manor and give the arrangements the benefit of your artistic eye then.' He'd made it clear to everyone that he wanted things immaculate for the visitors.

'I'd rather help Mum.' Rosamund looked down at the green peppers on her chopping board.

'Come on!' He tickled her in the ribs.

Rosamund leaned away, blushing unhappily and remembering the feeling of his arms pressing on her by the easel. She cut a pepper in half, exposing a row of pale seeds.

'Don't you like being tickled?' he teased. 'Look, Catherine doesn't mind!'

He pounced on Mum and tickled her waist till she dropped her mixing spoon.

'Off, or there won't be any dinner!' Mum cried, laughing. She tried to tickle him back, but he held her hands down and squeezed her into kissing position.

Rosamund concentrated on the chopping board.

When Richard went out, Mum scolded, 'Don't be such a bad sport.' She brushed messed-up curls away from her eyes.

'Mum!' murmured Rosamund, defending herself, wanting to go on and tell her how Richard acted in her room. She hadn't been able to tell her about the ghost yet either.

She needed Mum to stop being busy and listen. And to know Richard wouldn't burst in any second.

They heard him bellow for Sam to fetch some things and put them away. Mum clicked her tongue. She went to make sure he got on with it.

Sam had been in trouble again yesterday. Richard almost hit a spade when he drove the Porsche into the old stables.

'For heaven's sake be on your best behaviour tonight,' Mum told them when she plunked down an early supper of scrambled eggs. 'The Crosbys are important to Richard's business.'

'I'll be a cherub,' Sam reassured her, flapping arm wings behind him. 'But for your sake, not Sir Richardhead's.'

'*Sam*!'

'Cool it,' whispered Sam. 'Let his lordship sweat over his feast.'

Mum dashed up a quarter of an hour after people arrived to warn them to have everything tidy. Richard had started his tour.

She shouted to Sam from halfway up the tower steps and then tapped Rosamund's door. She had on a new slinky dress.

'Mum! You look terrific!' said Rosamund.

Mum smiled. 'I hope so. Richard puts so much store by entertaining.' She rushed back downstairs.

Immediately, Sam called, 'Ros, Ros, quick! Come up here!'

She found him feeling under his mattress. 'Homer's disappeared.'

'You idiot! Why did you have him out?'

'He never runs away now. Mum startled him when she shouted.'

'You shouldn't have risked it!'

'He's probably between the bed and the wall. Get

ready if he legs it.' He shifted the mattress.

'That's the stairs!' gasped Rosamund.

A noisy group came down the passage and went into her room.

'Blast. He's not back here,' said Sam. 'Perhaps he's in the bed. Probably wants a kip. I snitched a load of stuff from the cheese board for his supper.'

The voices hushed below. Richard was telling some story.

Rosamund eased back the duvet.

Sam lifted the bottom sheet. 'I think he's gone inside the mattress. He chewed a hole. Not to worry. He won't come out with all the yackety-yak.'

Hoots of laughter rose from downstairs.

Sam groaned. 'Oh, lords and ladies!'

A woman's voice rose up the stone spiral as they scrambled to tidy the bed. 'I didn't know we were going on an assault course. Don't know if I can manage this.'

'I'll give support from behind.'

'Don't you dare!'

Mrs Crosby emerged in a long flimsy dress. Richard followed, looking pleased with himself. Then up filed a young blonde woman, Mr Crosby, Mum and Howard Hunt.

The tower was packed. Hands protruded everywhere holding drinks.

'This is Rosamund,' said Richard. He put his free arm around her shoulder and squeezed as he introduced everyone. She hated the feel of his body.

58

'So it's your mysterious room we've just seen?' said Mr Crosby. 'It's very beautiful.'

'Thank you.' She edged away from Richard into the alcove.

'And this is Sam,' Mum said.

Sam gave everyone a courtly bow.

'I got bamboozled into letting that young man have this as his bedroom,' said Richard, sounding noble.

'Just the job,' said Mr Crosby. 'No unnatural visitors allowed up here, I bet.'

Mum glanced at Richard. She was annoyed about something.

'Have a look at that view,' said Richard. 'Isn't it superb?'

For a few moments, everyone oohed and leaned around each other's heads to see. Richard pointed out things exactly like a lord of the manor. It sounded as if the woods and fields were his too.

'Not much room, is there?' said Fran with the blonde hair, getting bored. She sat down on the edge of Sam's mattress.

'Good idea,' said Howard Hunt. Rosamund watched nervously as he lowered himself.

There was a scream. Homer shot past Fran's bare legs.

'A mouse!' she shrieked, leaping up.

'I'll catch him!' shouted Sam.

People jumped left and right to get out of the way. They yelled and bumped while Homer zigzagged between their feet. Drinks sprang from glasses and splashed clothes.

Mrs Crosby screeched as Homer fled up her long dress. He clung on waist high.

Mr Crosby shook the skirt. Homer leaped off.

'I think it's wet me!' gasped Mrs Crosby with horror.

Homer skimmed over the floorboards and out of the doorway. Sam dived after him. He scooped him off the steps and kept going.

'Ros, get a damp cloth from the bathroom!' cried Mum. She rushed to Mrs Crosby, apologising.

'Was that *his* mouse, Catherine?' Richard demanded.

Rosamund ran to fetch the cloth, glad to get away from Richard's angry face.

Chapter 8

The guests left soon after dinner. Rosamund dreaded what would happen. She tiptoed to the top of the staircase.

Mum came into the hallway and started upstairs. She looked done in.

'Ros!' she exclaimed when she saw her. 'Is Sam up there?'

'I think he's still outside.'

'He shouldn't be out this late! Richard's locked up.' She went into the gatehouse. She undid the lock and bolts and pulled open the heavy door.

Rosamund ran down and stood beside her. Their eyes searched the night, across the empty space that surrounded the manor to the deeper darkness of the lane wall on one side and the woods on the other.

Mum called, but there was no movement.

'Wretched boy!'

'Oh, Mum, don't be cross with him,' pleaded Rosamund. 'Homer got frightened and hid when you shouted about everyone coming up.'

'He shouldn't have had him loose with visitors in the house! Richard's in a terrible temper. Sam!' she yelled again.

She shoved the door together irritably. 'I'll have to try in a minute. You might as well come and help clear up since you're here. Be nice to Richard!'

Rosamund followed Mum into the kitchen tensely. She went straight to the sink and started washing pots.

Soon they heard Sam trying to nip upstairs. The Tudor burglar alarm gave him away.

Richard strode into the passage and roared, 'Sam! Come here!'

Sam shuffled in clutching an old biscuit tin. Rosamund's anxious eyes met his.

'Oh, Sam!' Mum cried.

'I'm sorry,' he said humbly.

Rosamund winced as Richard started shouting.

'You're sorry! You're sorry, and we're supposed not to mind! Do you realise your performance this evening has probably cost me thirty thousand pounds' worth of business?'

'No, surely –' interrupted Mum.

'Yes, thirty thousand, plus goodwill. Get in the real world, Catherine! Ann Crosby jolly near had a convulsion. And you can bet that dress was a designer label. She must absolutely love having it covered in mouse pee.'

Rosamund saw him glare at the tin held against Sam's T-shirt.

'Is it in there? Give it to me!'

'Why?'

'It's going in the stream. It's vermin!'

Rosamund gasped.

Sam made a break for the passage. Richard leaped on him. He tried to wrench the tin out of his hand.

The lid shot off and clattered onto the tiles. Homer jumped out. He belted through the dark opening into the wine-store. Sam tore after him.

'*Don't run in there*! Watch the Château –' There was an awesome crash as Sam fell over a clutch of wine standing near the door.

They all rushed to the doorway. When Richard switched on the light, Sam was picking himself off the flagstones with bottles rolling round him like ninepins.

'Sorry,' he said aghast.

Richard swore as he grovelled about retrieving and examining the wine bottles. Miraculously, none had broken.

'Get out, get out!' he bellowed when Sam tried to help. 'Let the mouse stay. I've got a trap set already.'

Rosamund saw a sickening wood and metal body-smasher baited in the corner.

'No, please!' begged Sam. 'I'll put him outside.'

'I don't want pests *anywhere* around the manor! Go!'

'I won't!'

'You will! Do I have to make you?' Richard stood up menacingly.

His bulk and height loured over Sam. Rosamund felt helpless. Beside her, Mum gripped the door jamb.

'You're a murderer!' yelled Sam.

'Come out,' ordered Mum, but Rosamund could tell that she was more alarmed than angry.

Sam looked at her, then back at Richard. 'You'll be sorry!'

He ran from the storeroom and through the kitchen. His eyes were full of tears.

Rosamund and Mum stood frozen while Richard put away the wine.

Mum said, 'He has been naughty, but I think trapping his mouse is going too far.'

'If he's had it loose once, he'll do it again!' barked Richard. 'Do you know how fast mice breed? Be reasonable, Catherine. We can't have vermin all over the place! They're a disgusting health hazard.'

He locked the door and dropped the key in his trouser pocket.

It took half an hour to clear up, but they hardly spoke. Rosamund's hands were shaking. How could someone want to kill a person's pet? It was horrible!

She mumbled goodnight. She didn't stop to kiss Mum in case Richard grabbed her as well.

She crept up the stone spiral and knocked on Sam's door.

He didn't respond. The tower room was quiet enough to be empty. Sam obviously felt too miserable to talk or even move.

Next morning, Rosamund heard Mum up there. 'Try and understand, darling. Richard sees it as pest control... Mice multiply so quickly...' Her voice petered out.

She added in desperation, 'I wasn't going to tell you now, but he said we might let you have a pedigree rabbit if you behave.'

64

'Tell the murderer to stuff his swanky rabbits!' shouted Sam.

'If you're going to take that attitude, I won't be able to persuade him to let your friends come again during the week.'

'In proper families, people's friends are always welcome!'

'You've broken a valuable window and wrecked important business entertaining,' said Mum.

'Yeah, well. I expect he'll set a person-trap soon to pest control me.'

Rosamund waited for Mum in the passage. As she came out of the tower, Sam's music exploded above, volume on max.

'Turn that down!' Mum shouted back up.

'He's impossible!' she snapped. Rosamund remembered the old amused way she used to say things like that.

'Has Richard been in the wine-store yet?' Rosamund whispered.

Mum pursed her lips. 'No.'

'Come in my room a minute,' Rosamund pleaded. 'I need to talk to you privately.'

'Not now!' Mum hurried off past the woodwormy beams.

'*Mum*!' Rosamund cried, but she was left standing alone by her bedroom door.

She stared across her room to the corner where she'd seen the first Rosamund. It was the most beautiful part of the room when the sun was out, but, on a grey day like today, it almost disappeared in shadow. She wished Rosamund were there with her now.

Suddenly, she knew what she would do. She ran downstairs after Mum.

'I'm going for a walk.'

'Fine,' answered Mum, as if she were glad not to be bothered anymore. Glad to be rid of her even. Mum was closed off inside herself a million miles away.

Rosamund walked along the footpath on the edge of the woods feeling very lonely.

On the other side of the stream, corn swayed under low clouds. It reminded her of the plaited corn carved on the mantelpiece in the big formal sitting room. She longed for their comfortable living room at Victoria Road where it was okay to just flop about.

She crossed a road and went up the church path. It curved through evergreens.

The church had been left unlocked after morning communion. A thick wooden door fitted a big arch like the door of the gatehouse and pushed open just as heavily.

She tiptoed up an aisle of box pews. She didn't know if she were looking for a plaque, a slab or a raised tomb, but somewhere in here Lucille had said Rosamund was buried.

She went round twice before she had the idea of looking under a piece of loose carpet near the chancel steps. Sure enough, it protected some brass memorials. She dragged the carpet away and knelt to study them.

A knight in one had a dog at his feet. Another man in a ruff had a row of his grieving children beneath him, segregated into girls on one side and boys on the other.

Then Rosamund saw the carving of a woman. Her pulse racing, she scrambled across to read the inscription:

HERE LYETH ROSAMUND THROKTON
DAVGHTER VNTO ANTONY WILLINGHAM
OF CLEVS ESQVIRE MARYED VNTO
THOMAS THROKTON OF –

She stopped reading and glanced up eagerly at the figure of the woman. A long gown. Hands in praying position. A smile. Head-dress back from the face.

Rosamund gulped. A shock wave charged through her.

She bent nearer. She ran a finger over the indentations of the woman's hair to make quite certain. The hair divided in front of the head-dress and was woven into plaits. They came down each side of the face and disappeared behind.

Rosamund touched the identical arrangement on her own head.

Slowly, she pulled the carpet back over the burial places. She walked dazedly past the box pews and out of the church.

What was happening? Had the first Rosamund given her the idea of wearing her hair this way? Had *she* made her ruin one picture and then helped her paint another brilliant one – a portrait of herself that, according to Richard, also looked like the second Rosamund?

A gap in the churchyard led to the ruins of the nunnery. She drifted through into a space enclosed by four walls, like Lucille's garden only much bigger. Bindweed with pale pink buds climbed the wall beside her like the plants on Lucille's trellises. Flowering purple valerian grew from nooks.

A single row of columns with arches above, perhaps part of a cloister walk, rose out of mown lawn. Mottled stones outlined the remains of the nuns' buildings. Rosamund slid down against one. She saw tiny multicoloured wild flowers growing among the blades of grass.

She slumped back, losing track of time. A swallow appeared out of the grey sky and dipped under a cloister arch. Rain began, big gentle drops.

Her thin top got clingy-wet, but she had no will to move. Nearby, the rain filled a hollow in a stone with clear musical notes over the rising and falling of the light wind.

She remembered the music she'd heard the first night at Cleaves. Women's voices rising softly – soothing, reassuring. She thought she could hear them again.

Nuns. Nuns singing without instruments. The women of this convent. Women who had taken Rosamund into their safe place when she was in trouble.

She felt comforted and able to go back.

Chapter 9

Homer was either very lucky or very clever. When Rosamund went down to the kitchen after changing her clothes, Mum whispered that the trap had gone off, but hadn't caught him. Richard had reset it.

The two of them scuttled about putting out last night's leftovers for lunch, not wanting to listen, but listening, for the distant snap of metal. Mum didn't even notice Rosamund's wet hair.

Hunger drove Sam downstairs. He was wearing his cotton jacket.

Richard ignored him, but rattled the storeroom door unnecessarily when he unlocked to get wine for lunch. He switched on the light and kicked the door shut behind him in case Homer was nearby.

'Assassin!' muttered Sam.

Mum didn't say anything.

'Catherine!' Richard called sharply. He came out. 'Have you been going through the wine?'

'No.'

'It's in all the wrong places. I had the Latour on the left and the Pomerol at the bottom.'

'I expect you moved them when you were sorting out the wines last night.'

'I didn't!' Richard glowered at Sam. 'Have you been in here after that mouse?'

'Am I supposed to have magicked the door open?' inquired Sam.

'Cut that cheekiness or you can jolly well go back upstairs without anything to eat!'

'Go and wash your hands, Sam,' said Mum. 'Your nails have enough dirt in them to start a garden.'

'I'm not going to take rudeness, Catherine,' Richard said as Sam went.

'It's the trap!' Mum replied frostily.

Later in the afternoon, Rosamund began to sniffle. She must have caught cold in the rain. Going to pile on more clothes, she heard Mum and Richard arguing in their bedroom. She thought Mum might be insisting that Richard stop trying to kill Homer, but the argument seemed to be about the agency.

Rosamund wondered for the first time if marrying Richard were really going to be that great for Mum.

She had met him seven months ago when the agency started supplying staff for his company. He'd come on a million times stronger than any of her other men friends. He wasn't a man to accept a No.

Rosamund remembered one night soon after he and Mum started seeing each other. Mum said on the phone that she really must stay in and finish some work. Richard turned up anyway.

'Twenty minutes to get ready. We've got a booking at the Mill. Don't let me down. I had to bribe the head waiter to get a table tonight.'

Mum laughed, flattered and bewildered, looking very

pretty with her hair falling about in long untidy curls. 'But I haven't arranged anything for the children.'

'Children! This charming young lady is nearly old enough to be a baby-sitter herself,' Richard told her. 'I'll bring you back before they turn into pumpkins.'

If that was supposed to be midnight, they didn't make it. Rosamund heard the front door open and, after stiffening for a moment until she heard Mum's voice, switched on her torch and looked at the time. It was half past two.

When Richard wanted something, he went for it. He outbid everyone to get Cleaves, and then decided moving in together was the perfect way to start a marriage. Everything happened so fast that it felt as if they were still catching their breaths.

Sam came haring down the passage after Rosamund.

'Have I got news! Can I come in?'

She left her door open for him and went to get a sweatshirt. He dashed through and scanned the room. He saw the spoilt picture leaning against the wall.

'Oh! Do you know already?'

'Know what?'

'Your room's haunted! Is that a ghost you've painted?'

Rosamund stopped with her sweatshirt half on. 'Why do you think it's haunted?'

'I just heard that Crosby geezer on the answer phone. Said next time they'd cut the spook and rodent tour. SR told them last night that this room was locked up when he bought Cleaves because someone had seen a ghost in it.'

'You mean Mum knows too? She put me in here without saying anything!'

'SR probably hypnotised her. Bet he'd be petrified of having a haunted room.'

Rosamund went silent. Numbly, she shoved her arms into the sweatshirt. The room hadn't been a wonderful gift. She'd been used to get rid of something suspect.

'I'd love a spooky room, but the tower's even better.' Sam bounced on the bed. 'This place is too much for SR. He thinks he's lord of the manor, but he can't catch Homer!'

Rosamund looked at him. She felt worse. Last night Homer was stuffed with dinner party cheese, but the bait on the trap was bound to tempt him soon.

Sam darted over and picked up the spoilt picture. 'You haven't really seen this, have you?'

Rosamund shook her head. 'Not that.' She pointed to the easel. 'But I think I've seen her.'

Rosamund's nose was running the next day. Mum felt her forehead when she came back late from the agency.

'I think you've got a fever. Better go to bed and sleep it off. Have you had something to eat?'

Rosamund snuffled. 'I'm not hungry.'

'You should have a lot of liquid. I'll bring you up a drink later.'

She gave Rosamund a little kiss in the middle of her parting. It made Rosamund hope that when they were alone upstairs, Mum would at last be in a mood to listen.

It seemed ages until she remembered her promise. Rosamund dozed off and woke as daylight was fading. She turned over when she heard the door.

The steaming mug wasn't carried by Mum, but by Richard.

'I'm sorry the manor's miss is under the weather. Jolly bad luck,' he said. He pushed the door shut behind him with his foot.

'Is Mum coming?' asked Rosamund anxiously.

'Buried in agency accounts. Worked to a frazzle. You must help persuade her to let me make things easier.' He put down the mug and sat on the edge of the bed. 'How are you feeling, love?'

'It's only a cold.' Actually, she felt awful. She ached all over and her forehead had begun to throb.

Richard stroked her hair. When she moved her head away, his hand slid under the duvet and stroked her bare arm.

'I'll be fine,' said Rosamund. 'Thanks for bringing the drink.'

She wished she hadn't changed into her nightie. Otherwise, she could have got out of bed and pretended to need to go to the bathroom.

'Catherine decided on lemon tea. I hope you like that.'

If Mum had made the drink, she can't have been that buried in accounts. Richard must have intercepted it. Rosamund felt cheated and suddenly tearful. She wanted Mum!

'Shall I help you sit up?' coaxed Richard.

'I'll let it cool a bit. Could you ask Mum to come up as soon as she can, please?' The *please* came out with the caught hiccup of a sob.

'Oh, sweetie! You're feeling absolutely rotten! Come on, give me a hug.'

Richard leaned over and pushed a hand under each side of her back to pull her against him. She smelled wine.

He clamped her against his huge body. She felt smothered. She wriggled, but he clung on. All at once, she was frightened of him.

He sat up. The door opened. Mum!

'How is she? Goodness, it's getting dark.' Mum came over and switched on the bedside lamp, very businesslike. 'I wondered about some aspirins.'

Richard stayed sitting on the bed. 'She says she's only feeling a bit coldy.'

Mum perched a hand on his shoulder. Rosamund decided they'd made it up.

'All right then, darling,' said Mum. 'A good night's sleep is what you need. We'll leave you in peace. Don't forget your drink.'

Mum bent and kissed her. 'I must remember to see about your curtains sometime. Night, night.'

Richard put an arm round Mum's waist. They walked towards the door together.

Now Rosamund felt angry. Why didn't Mum remember that she wanted to talk to her? And why didn't she understand that Richard shouldn't come into her room, shouldn't *touch* her?

Her body ached so that she could hardly lean on an elbow to sip the lemon tea. When she switched off the lamp, moonlight flung the outline of the window over the room again. The moon was a bright threequarters full and, between the arches, the leading traced an irregular net.

Rosamund couldn't remember dropping off to sleep, but suddenly it was the middle of the night. Something dreadful was happening in the room.

Screams pierced the semi-darkness. The first Rosamund was cowering where the easel should stand. A man in a loose robe leaned over her, gripping her shoulders and shaking her viciously.

The first Rosamund wrenched away and fled down the room. The man chased her. She shouted at him. '*No!*' She threw something brass and shining. A candlestick.

It soared in terrifying slow motion over Rosamund's bed and crashed through the window. The sound of shattering glass turned the screams into a desperate wail. Splinters of glass hailed down, jagged, hurting, cruel.

The light snapped on. Mum ran across the room in her nightdress, followed by Richard in a dressing gown with bare legs, and then Sam in boxer shorts.

Rosamund sat up and pulled the duvet round her. She poured with sweat, shivering at the same time so that her teeth bumped together.

Mum held her. 'Whatever's the matter? We could hear you right round the front.'

75

'It wasn't me!'

'It was, darling. You must have had a nightmare.' She felt Rosamund's forehead. 'Oh, Ros! You're burning! I'll get something to get that fever down.'

Rosamund grabbed her. 'Don't go!'

'I'll stay with you,' said Richard.

'*Mum!*' pleaded Rosamund.

'Would you get the aspirins from our bathroom cupboard?' Mum asked Richard. 'Sam, go and get some water, please.'

When they left, Rosamund buried her face in Mum's shoulder. 'Tell Richard not to come back in,' she begged.

'Don't be silly,' said Mum, stiffening a little. 'He's concerned about you.'

'Can I have a lock on my door?'

'Of course not. It would be a fire hazard.'

'Oh, Mum!' Rosamund started to cry.

'There,' said Mum more softly. 'Some nasty dream's frightened you. Let me straighten those sheets. Look, you're completely untucked underneath.'

'Mum, this room is *haunted*!'

'Who's been telling you that?'

'I've seen a ghost. There were two in here just now. Mum, *you know about it*!'

'Did you hear Richard when he was showing the guests around?'

'No, but Sam heard Mr Crosby say.'

'Oh, honestly! I was annoyed Richard repeated that

story, but he couldn't resist. That's all it is. A good story.'

'Rosamund's ghost lives in here. It's her room.'

'Darling,' said Mum, looking at her anxiously. 'You're Rosamund.'

'The first Rosamund. She lived at Cleaves in the sixteenth century. Her father did out this room specially for her.'

'How do you know?'

'Lucille told me.'

'Ah.' Mum smiled. 'Lucille's a dear, but she's as besotted with Cleaves as Richard is. I expect she'd love a story about a romantic ghost. She won't believe it really.'

'She hasn't mentioned ghosts at all! She just told me the history. About Rosamund and the cousin who got at her. Mum, how could you put me in here and not say anything?'

'Because ghosts only exist in people's minds. They see them when they get nervous or worked up. Like you are now,' she added as Richard came back in with the tablets.

'She's heard the story,' Mum told him tightly. 'She thinks she's seeing ghosts.'

'Poor love!' crooned Richard. 'I'll load a gun and keep guard, shall I?'

'Don't tease. She's not well.'

Sam arrived with the water. Mum dropped the soluble aspirins into the glass.

'Seriously,' said Richard. 'I'd be glad to sit up with her.'

Panic swept through Rosamund. 'I'm okay now.'

'Yes,' agreed Mum, 'of course you are, darling. It's the fever upsetting you.'

It's not just the fever! Rosamund wanted to shout. It's *him.* He's like Rosamund's cousin! But she had to drink the medicine and let Mum go.

She reached for her rabbit by the side of the pillow and pressed it close.

Chapter 10

Mum hurried in with a thermometer in the morning, wondering if she should ring the doctor. They always caused trouble for Mum when they were sick. She needed to be at the agency every day.

Being away for the honeymoon must have piled up tons of work. Rosamund guessed that Mum didn't want to complain, because then Richard would go on about joining the business with his.

Rosamund felt less achy, but exhausted. Mum was satisfied when she found that her temperature was right down.

She dashed over and asked Lucille to look in later. She told her that Rosamund had been feverish in the night. Lucille's immediate sympathetic nods made her suspect that she'd heard the commotion.

Halfway through the morning, a knock sounded outside Rosamund's room. 'May a page and an old dame come in?' called a gentle voice.

The biggest, most magnificent bouquet of flowers Rosamund had ever seen appeared around the door. Already arranged in a tall vase were lilies, carnations and pink, white and Rosa mundi roses. Sam marched forward, carrying them in front of him like a trophy.

'Oh!' gasped Rosamund 'Are they all for me?'

'Who else, my dear?' said Lucille, following him.

'Now where would you like them? Don't sit up. What about in the corner where you can see them from the pillow?'

Sam ceremoniously settled the vase in front of the panels. He bowed to Rosamund. 'At your service, my lady.'

He paced sedately to the door, and then could be heard charging along the passage and hurtling downstairs. Rosamund and Lucille smiled at each other.

Lucille said kindly, 'How is it then?'

The question seemed to refer not just to the chill, but to everything. Rosamund didn't know how to answer.

Lucille smiled again, seeming to understand. She walked peacefully up the room and studied the coloured fragments of glass under the stone arches.

'My goodness. There *are* painted lines. That certainly is a petal. Isn't it wonderful how you never get to the end of the mysteries of an old house!'

'I'm afraid I only have my painting chair to ask you to sit on,' said Rosamund.

'I like an upright chair, dear. Thank you.' Lucille turned the chair towards the bed, her cheerful straw hat dipping and giving a view of the cherries and handmade flowers as she sat down. She didn't look at the picture on the easel.

'The room seems very happy with your things in it. It's a sort of day and night chamber for you as it was for the first Rosamund, isn't it? You do your painting here. She probably did embroidery.'

'Would people have just come in and out as they wanted, or would it have been private?'

'Going into a person's bedchamber should need an invitation,' said Lucille very definitely.

'But sometimes it's hard to stop people coming in your room, especially if you don't have a lock on the door.'

Lucille looked into her eyes as if she had all the time in the world to listen to whatever she might say.

After a moment, Rosamund asked, 'Do you think the window could have been broken from inside, perhaps because the first Rosamund threw something at her cousin when he was in here? When he was trying to make her marry him?'

'That's quite possible.'

Rosamund wanted to tell her that she'd been shown what happened. But the being shown was mixed up with Richard. She couldn't talk about that.

'Do you think my painting might look like the first Rosamund?' she asked instead.

Lucille turned to the easel. 'Oh, yes, dear!' she exclaimed. 'How beautifully you've caught her!'

Rosamund swallowed. 'Am I like her? I went to the church, you see, and in the brass memorial she's got plaits.' Her voice hushed. 'I didn't start wearing my hair like that till I came here.'

Lucille nodded. 'Wouldn't you like to be like the first Rosamund? She's often encouraged me. I wonder how unusual she was for her time in believing that her body and mind belonged to her.'

Light shimmered on the flowers in the corner. Their scent drifted about the room, carrying Lucille's words.

'Lucille?'

'Yes, dear?'

'The first Rosamund is still here, isn't she?'

'In some way, I believe she may be,' said Lucille. 'When she's needed.'

After Mum rang at lunch time, Sam brought up a bowl of soup on a tray. He was filthy. Rosamund wondered if he were back on archaeological research, but felt too tired to try and get anything out of him.

She slept again in the afternoon and woke dying of thirst. She sat up and drank almost the whole bottle of mineral water Mum had left by the bed.

'Report from the tower,' Sam called from the passage. 'SR's back.'

He was early.

'Sam, come in here please! He's bound to come up.'

Sam stood in the doorway. He had put on his cotton jacket again, although the sun was out. 'No thanks. I'm not into voluntary parleys.'

'He'll go away if we're doing something. Get the draughts. They're in that box by the easel.'

Sam grinned. 'Only if you promise to make the ghost appear while I'm here.'

'Sam, *please*!'

'Oh, all right. Suppose we've got to humour the Lady Rosamund when she's indisposed.' He rummaged out the game and sat cross-legged on the floor by the bed.

They put the board on a pillow between them. Sam expertly spread the draughts so it looked as if they were in the middle of playing.

He chuckled. 'These are ones I've taken. I'm winning.'

When Richard came in, they pretended to be working out their next moves.

'How are you, sweetie?' he asked. 'I've been jolly worried about you.' He felt her forehead.

'Scuse!' said Sam. He reached over with a grimy hand and jumped a row of Rosamund's pieces.

'Perhaps you should let your sister rest,' said Richard gruffly.

'Oh, I'm much better, thank you,' Rosamund said, and realised that, apart from a stuffed-up nose, she really was.

'Lord – whoops, I mean *king* – please,' demanded Sam.

Rosamund made his draught into a double.

'Best of five games, huh?' said Sam. 'Give you a chance to make a comeback.'

Richard frowned, but retreated. 'Call me if you need anything, love,' he said to Rosamund.

'I won't, but thanks,' she answered brightly. She felt as if they were acting parts, being polite and ordinary after the way he'd grabbed her last night.

They heard him clack down the stairs.

Sam rolled his eyes. 'Sweetie! Lays it on thick for you, doesn't he?'

Rosamund wondered if she could tell Sam about the way he acted when no one else was there. She decided she would feel too embarrassed.

'Let's be having this ghost then,' Sam said. He addressed the room. 'Oh, Rosamund the First, reveal thyself to an humble yeo-person!'

'She's not going to show just to be gawked at,' said Rosamund. 'She was here last night...or...some memory of hers was here.'

'Is that why you were screaming?'

'She was screaming. A man was threatening her. I think it was her cousin. Lucille says he tried to force her to marry him.'

'Did she escape or get lock-wed?'

'Escape, but I don't know how. I wish I did. The cousin pushed in and lived at the manor after her father died. She must have got away when he wasn't expecting it.'

She stared at Sam. 'Something's moving inside your jacket!'

'Blast, does he show? Lucky SR didn't notice.'

'Does what show?'

He pointed a finger at her. 'No letting on.' He unzipped the jacket's front pocket. A little head popped out.

'Homer! He's all right!' Rosamund whispered ecstatically.

'Of course, he's all right. You didn't think I was going to let him get poleaxed, did you?'

Sam held an arm against his body. Homer jumped on. He explored the air with quick head turns, sniffing in every direction. Rosamund looked at the shining dark beads of eyes, the sensitive ears, the soft fur. The thought of metal jaws crushing all that life was too awful for words.

'I'll have to keep him in the side pocket. Pity. He likes to hear my heart beat.'

'Can he breathe in those pockets?'

'Yeah, look. They're lined with this holey stuff like in swimming trunks. If he didn't like it, he'd soon chew his way out.'

'And you've been going on to Mum about the trap as if he were still in danger!'

'He *is* still in danger if Sir Richardhead gets hold of him. She mustn't suspect. She's under his power. She'd never have let anyone hurt Homer if I'd had him before.'

'Did you nick the key?'

'No chance. His lordship keeps it on him all the time. Needs constant access to his supply.'

'Did he get out by himself then?'

'Maybe.'

'Come on!'

Sam grinned. 'I was in there as soon you lot were in beddy-byes Saturday night. The wine got a little mixed-up while I was searching.'

'How did you get in?'

'There's a ventilation grille in the outside wall. The mortar's dodgy.' He chuckled. 'I loosened it with the *jolly useful* penknife SR gave me.'

'Why hasn't he guessed?'

'It's under that table with the old beer crates, and it looks small.'

'But you couldn't get downstairs and outside without them hearing. Sam! Have you found a secret way out?'

'It's better you don't know.'

'I need to know! I'm living in a haunted room! You don't know what might help me.' It wasn't ghosts she wanted to avoid. It was Richard.

Mum wouldn't let her get up the rest of the day, but when Rosamund begged, she did bring up her supper herself. She looked tired. Rosamund felt guilty.

'I'm going to sleep as soon as I'm finished, so I'll be completely better tomorrow,' Rosamund said.

'That's a good idea,' said Mum.

'I don't want a drink or anything. Will you tell the others not to disturb me? You'll tell Richard?'

'Oh, Ros. Please don't make things more difficult by taking against him. You'll hurt his feelings, and then he'll be harder on Sam. I know the business about the mouse seems cruel, but he doesn't see things the way we do. He doesn't understand.'

'Why can't you make him understand? And it isn't just Homer – '

'*Ros*! Please!' Mum cried. She raked her hand through her hair as if she had a hundred problems and couldn't cope.

Rosamund saw that she would have to go on waiting for the right time to talk to her.

Chapter 11

Everyone was in the kitchen next morning when Richard unlocked the wine-store and went to check the trap.

They heard the light click on. Then Richard yelped as if he'd been bitten. He jumped back through the doorway.

'What's the matter?' said Mum.

Rosamund knew she was afraid Richard was going to produce Homer's mangled body. But it couldn't be that. She moved so that she could see into the storeroom.

'Cripes!' she gasped.

In the rack against the white-washed wall, brown bottle bottoms massed together to form the clear and quite terrifying shape of a monster mouse. It glared out of a round eye of white bottle bottoms with a single startling red bottle top in the centre.

For a second, the shock paralysed Richard. He gawped with open mouth.

His eyes fled to discarded bottles on the floor and back to the monster. Then he lunged at Sam.

'*You* did this, didn't you?' he yelled. '*Didn't* you?' He seized hold of him.

Mum rushed over and grabbed Richard's arm. He let go. Sam darted to the other side of the kitchen table.

'How *dare* you tamper with my wine?' Richard bellowed.

'How am I supposed to have done anything?' asked Sam.

'Who's done it then?'

'I'd say the only person who could get into a windowless locked room would be a ghost. We know *one* room in the manor is haunted. Perhaps ghosts spread to places where they don't like what's going on.'

'Cut that rubbish!' Richard yelled. 'I know it was you!'

He strode to the door and examined the lock.

'You went in to get a bottle about eleven o'clock last night,' Mum said. 'Sam was already upstairs.'

Richard slammed the door and relocked it. 'I can't deal with this nonsense now!' he snarled. They listened to his angry footsteps strike the stone flags all the way up the passage.

'Sam?' Mum asked severely.

Sam shrugged.

For a second, Rosamund thought Mum was going to blow her top. Then she turned abruptly and went off tight-lipped to get ready for work.

As soon as Mum and Richard were gone, Rosamund ran up to the tower. She heard Sam's music from the steps. He sat on the mattress stroking Homer with a finger.

He chuckled as she came in. 'Don't think the lord likes his treasure store being haunted, do you?'

She had to hand it to him. 'You're brilliant!' She sat down slowly so as not to frighten Homer. 'The trouble is, Mum's upset as well.'

'I know. I'm sorry, but it isn't just this. SR is putting the screws on about taking over the agency. Howard Hunt was asking on the answer phone when they're going to start the paperwork.'

'Does Mum realise he's counting on her giving in?'

'I tried to tell her, but she won't let me say anything about SR. She went mad when she heard I'd touched his answer phone. Want some breakfast now it's safe?' he asked Homer.

He took him over to the cage. The door stood wide open.

'I've got to keep this looking empty for a while,' he explained. 'That's why I carry Homer about in my jacket when Mum and SR are here. Later on, I'll turn it round the other way. Make it seem like I'm using it for a stool.'

He tipped some muesli into Homer's food bowl. The little mouse scampered across to eat.

'Sam, please tell me how you get outside.'

'Hmm.' Sam considered while he emptied Homer's water out of a tower window. He poured fresh water from a bottle.

'All right. But you're not even to hint to anyone. If Mum found out, I'd get evicted from here for sure.'

'I promise.'

Laughing excitedly as if he'd been longing to show her all the time, Sam bounded to the alcove. He moved his cricket bat and whisked away a pile of clothes.

'First we unplug the magic hole.' He deftly pulled a slice of wine cork from a chink in the edge of a wide floorboard which crossed the alcove. He stuck his finger in the hole and jiggled, digging at the same time with the fingertips of his other hand.

'And, hey presto!' The board flipped up. He lifted it away. Then he took out the board right under the window as well.

Rosamund crawled over and peered into darkness. She breathed up must and damp air. Sam clicked on his bicycle lamp and shone it down an awesome vertical stone shaft.

'*Wow*!' Rosamund exclaimed. 'How did you find it?'

'Homer showed me. He stuck his head in the hole. When I went to plug it, I couldn't feel anything underneath. I prised up the board and had a look.'

'What is it? A well or some sort of torture pit?'

'It's the lav.'

'What?'

'The garderobe. The alcove probably had a stone seat. The plonkers dropped down the shaft and out a shoot into the moat.'

'It must have stunk!'

Sam grinned. 'They probably gave it the odd sluice. But look! You haven't noticed the best bit. Someone's made a way to get down!'

He shone the torch on an iron rung about half a metre from the top. Others were hammered in below making a ladder similar to the one that had gone up to the roof.

'Yuk! Who'd want to climb down inside a toilet?'

'Right on. It must have been an escape route. Perhaps your ghost used it when she was a person.'

'*Maybe*! She'd have had to get out of her room without her cousin noticing, but then it would be just up the tower. Are you sure it's still safe? You could kill yourself falling down there.'

'I had to be careful the first time, but Will was here. The rungs are rock solid. The whole thing's built in the thickness of the wall.'

'What happens at the bottom?'

'The shoot exit got buried when the moat was filled in. We've cleared it. It's behind those bushes at the bottom of the tower. You can squeeze under and get out.'

'You'd have had to swim the moat when you got down, wouldn't you?'

'Yep, or just sit it out in the bottom of the shaft and hope no one had to go.'

Rosamund giggled. 'Don't! Show me where it comes out.'

'Okay. We can leave the boards off now we're on our own.' He picked up the bicycle lamp and his school tie.

As they went along the moat dip, Sam pointed to an innocent-looking ventilation grille near where the tower joined on to the kitchen. 'There's where I get into the wine-store.'

'That is small!' said Rosamund.

'I know. It's incredible what a little space you can get through if you hunch up your shoulders.'

He'd worked the metal grid in and out carefully and rubbed dirt into a few scratch marks on the stones. Anybody would have to inspect really closely to notice any tampering.

They pushed on behind the bushes to the excavation site. Some of the bushes were rather wilted.

Sam and Will had dug a trench along part of the tower wall. A rectangle like an empty window space had appeared at the new ground level.

Rosamund looked up the tower and saw that the shaft exited directly below the alcove window. It must run all the way down two floors inside that blind wall.

'Gosh.'

'Fantastic, huh? It was hard work digging it out, I can tell you.'

'Let's have the lamp.'

Rosamund stuck her head and the hand holding the lamp into the hole.

Stale dank air filled the shaft. The temperature dropped at least ten degrees. The lamp shone on pitted surfaces of stone. Further up she saw the outline of the iron footholds.

She ducked back outside.

'Going to try it?' asked Sam.

'Well ... ' She wasn't keen. But if the first Rosamund had used it, she ought to be able to.

'I can't hold the lamp and climb. How am I going to see?'

'Head gear.' Sam held up his school tie which had reorganised itself into a grubby snake. 'Tie round the head. Lamp on the tie. 'Course with you we could probably clip the lamp straight on to those plaits.'

'No thanks. I'll have the tie.'

He knotted it round her head, then fastened the bicycle lamp on her forehead.

'Good as a caver,' he said, pronouncing it in mock French to rhyme with halver.

'Okay then. Keep back. Don't block the air.'

'Can't fuss about air quality in a lav. But don't worry. I haven't used it since last night.'

'Sam!'

'I didn't! Go on.'

Rosamund eased under and wriggled until she was sitting in the bottom of the shaft. She drew her arms up close to her body to find the first iron rung. It was ice-cold. She sneezed.

She pulled herself to standing position.

There was just enough room, but she felt horribly constricted. The cold rough stones grazed her arms as she climbed. It seemed as if years and years of winter frost had stored up inside the wall.

'*Ooooo! Helloooo!*'

'Stop it, Sam!'

She heard his chuckle. 'You okay?' he called.

'Freezing! '

She hated her face being so close to the wall. She could almost taste it. A musty stink filled her nose and caught in her throat. She wanted to spit.

She remembered stories about people being sealed up inside walls. Discovered hundreds of years after. How could anyone be so cruel as to do that? How could they just scrub out what it felt like to be the other person?

Then stories came back about tunnels and secret rooms being made. Priest holes. During Elizabeth I's time. But that was at the end of the sixteenth century, after Rosamund. This escape route might not have even existed when she needed it!

The thought was a letdown. But it could have been made as an escape way when Cleaves was a fortified medieval manor, *before* Rosamund lived. You just didn't know.

Her nose ran and dripped, but she didn't dare let go to wipe it.

As she got nearer the top, she could hear Sam's tape still playing. The lively beat danced encouragingly down the shaft.

Sam had run back through the house and was waiting at the top.

'Way to go!' he enthused as she hauled herself out.

She pulled off the headband. 'Give me a tissue quick.' She blew out dirty snot.

'How d'you like it?'

Rosamund looked down the sheer black drop. She could hardly believe that she'd braved it. She wouldn't have, if it hadn't been for Rosamund.

'It wasn't exactly fun, but I'm glad I managed,' she said. 'Thanks for showing me.'

She was sure Rosamund would have used this way if she could have. How she actually escaped remained another of Cleaves' secrets.

Chapter 12

When Rosamund was emptying Lucille's flower vase, Mum came in the kitchen to make coffee.

'I'm going to Manchester tomorrow,' she said. 'Interviews.' Sometimes she had to travel to find new people for the agency register.

'What time will you get back?' asked Rosamund uneasily.

'I'll have to stay the night, worst luck. Three of them can't see me until after work.'

'Can we go to Aunt Susie's?'

'Richard will be here.' Mum bustled about tidying while she waited for the kettle to boil.

'Do you have to go?'

'Don't start, darling. You know I have to keep the agency running smoothly.'

'I don't want to be here without you.'

'Come on, you're used to it now.'

Rosamund swallowed, feeling panicky. 'Please, I don't want to stay with Richard. Mum, listen!'

But Mum was suddenly impatient. She banged a cupboard shut.

'Are you and Sam plotting to wreck everything? Just try harder to get on with Richard! Can't you help me make our new life work? You're being very selfish!'

Rosamund felt as if she'd been slapped. Was Richard

the only one who mattered to Mum now?

She went to return the vase. She told herself that Mum was tense about keeping control of the agency. Mum just wanted them all to make a good family.

She wondered if she were being selfish. Perhaps Richard hadn't done anything very bad. Perhaps she should put up with him for Mum's sake.

Her stomach clenched at the thought of going on dodging him. She'd managed to keep him out of her room in the last week by staying on the alert. If he were about by himself, she went and did something near Sam, but she had this sickening edgy feeling that he knew why.

Birds called in the enclosed garden. They'd been taking evening dips in the birdbath.

Jasmine gave a sweet scent by the door, but Lucille was out. Rosamund had to leave the vase on the step.

The next day, Rosamund decided she'd offer to play cricket with Sam after supper. They could stay outside until dark, and then it would be bedtime.

When Richard came back, she heard him talking to Sam at the end of the passage. It didn't sound like trouble, so she stayed in her room.

Five minutes later, Sam called, 'Ros, I'm going to Will's.' He rapped on the door.

She dived to open it. 'Since when?'

'SR's going to the wine merchant's. He's taking me. Will said I can stay the night.'

'You can't leave me here by myself!' she whispered urgently.

'Yeah, bit grim,' he whispered in agreement. 'Oh, blast. You want me to stay?'

He *had* to! How could she explain why she needed him so badly? She wished she'd tried to tell him about Richard before.

'Is Julie still on holiday?' Sam asked.

'Hey, no. They'll be back.'

'You could ask her to come. Mum won't mind.'

'Yes...' Julie did want to come over straight away.

'Is that okay then?'

Rosamund's heart was still thumping, but she didn't want to disappoint Sam for nothing. She nodded.

'Great! Check in the morning Homer's got water, will you? The safe's turned round and disguised, but distract SR if he goes up there nosing.'

'Can't you take Homer to Will's?'

'Two cats and no cage for when we're asleep.'

'Are you ready, Sam?' Richard called up the stairs. 'Tell Rosamund I won't be long.'

'Fare thee well, sweet lady,' said Sam, dropping the whispering. He made his courtly bow and raced down the passage. Rosamund stared after him.

It'll be all right, she told herself. Richard will keep away if Julie's about.

As soon as the gatehouse door clunked, she ran down to the kitchen phone. She pressed Julie's number.

Rob answered after one ring.

'Hi, it's Rosamund,' she said. Her body slackened with relief. 'Did you have a good holiday?'

'Terrific! How are things at the great house?'

'Fine, thanks. I'm ringing to see if Julie would like to come for the night.'

'I know she'd jump at it if she were here, but the friends we were sharing the cottage with are renting another week. They asked her to stay on. A jammy Joe, isn't she?'

Oh, no, no, no!

'I'll get her to phone you next Wednesday,' Rob continued cheerfully. 'All right?'

'Yes,' Rosamund mumbled. Not all right! she screamed inside. If only she could just tell Rob. *I'm alone with my stepfather, and I'm frightened.*

Instead, she said politely, 'Thank you. 'Bye then.'

'Jammy Joe' Rob had called Julie. The same expression Julie used. Because it was a family expression. Why hadn't Mum married someone like Rob? *Why had she left her alone?*

Rosamund searched Mum's phone book and found the number of her other good friend from school.

No one answered.

What about Aunt Susie? Ask if she would come and get her.

But Aunt Susie would want to know why. She'd have to tell her she didn't like being alone with Richard. Mum would be cross.

She got out the frozen stuff they were supposed to

have for supper and put it in the oven. She laid the table.

She decided to ring Mum's mobile. It was only taking messages. She hesitated, wondering what could she say with Mum all hassled by work that would make any difference. No words came. She hung up.

She stayed by the phone and kept pressing her school friend's number, listening to some rings, clicking off and then trying again. It was useless, but her mind was in a panic, unable to think of anything better to do.

Her stomach drew tight when she heard Richard come back. He entered the kitchen jovially, carrying a case of wine.

'That looks super. Good girl,' he said, surveying the table. He patted her arm before unlocking the wine-store.

He had dismembered the monster mouse the day after it appeared, but for some reason hadn't set the trap again.

'He's not *quite* sure it was me!' Sam chortled to Rosamund. 'Look how he reaches round to switch the light on now before he goes in.'

Rosamund got the food out of the oven. Richard came to the table with a bottle and some glasses. She saw that he expected her to serve him the same way Mum did.

She heaped his plate. The amount he ate still astonished her.

'I've opened some Chablis,' he said. 'An elegant wine for an elegant lady.'

'No, really. I'm not that keen on wine.'

'But you must try this. I put it in the fridge this morning to get it just right.' He poured her a glass. 'Now, come on. Tell me what you think.'

Rosamund took a sip. Richard watched her expectantly, so she said, 'You probably get used to it.'

He roared with laughter. 'You get to love it!' he boomed. 'You're sipping the cost of a loaf of bread with every mouthful.'

'Oh, save it for Mum!'

'There's plenty more for Catherine. We're going to enjoy this lovely bottle ourselves.' He reached over and squeezed her hand.

Rosamund blushed.

Richard finished a roll and buttered another. 'You know, you're turning into a jolly stunning young lady. I'm not sure you're not going to be more of a beauty than your mother, as they say.'

Rosamund stared at her plate.

'And how are the wonderful creations going? When am I going to get my picture? What a jolly lucky miss you are. Gorgeous and talented!' He watched her as he ate. 'But so serious. Come on, give me a smile!'

She tried faintly so that he would stop teasing. He laughed, very pleased.

The meal seemed to go on forever, but it would be rude to leave the table before he'd finished.

'Drink up!' he urged. 'You're letting me drink the whole bottle.'

Mum had bought a sticky toffee pudding. Rosamund

couldn't face it. She nibbled a pear. Richard wanted two large helpings of pudding.

At last, she was able to clear. Richard handed her his plate to put in the dishwasher. When she straightened up, he suddenly wrapped his arms round her.

'Thank you for looking after me so well,' he said. He held her against him all the way down her body like he did to Mum. But she wasn't Mum. He shouldn't do it to her.

She pulled away. He emptied the last of the Chablis into his glass.

'Going to watch television?' he asked.

If she did, he might come and sit by her. 'I'm in the middle of a book,' she said.

He followed her up the passageway and went to the library. There could be no sneaking out of the gatehouse.

When she reached the oak finial at the bottom of the staircase, he called, 'I'll look in and say goodnight later.'

'Oh, don't bother. I'm fine.'

'Catherine would like me to.'

If he wanted to come into her room, there was no way she could stop him. Now her stomach felt as if a claw were gripping inside.

The only way to get away from him would be to climb down the garderobe while he was in the library. She could hide in the stables or the woods, even crouch in the bottom of the shaft all night if necessary.

But he'd try to find her. He'd tell Mum he'd been worried, and then Mum would be furious. She wouldn't believe he'd pinned her up against him like she was his girlfriend. Mum had decided she and Sam had a pact to make trouble.

'*Mum! Mum!*' she whispered desperately, as if she were pleading with her.

She stood helplessly in her room. It wasn't Mum's fault. It was Richard who forced himself on her, pretending he didn't know she hated it.

She lifted the spoilt painting of the girl surrounded by darkness. A body with nothing inside. She thought, it's like that. People can do what they like if they pretend you're blank inside.

She walked around the easel and looked at the first Rosamund. She had refused to be treated as a blank. She knew she was a person. When someone tried to force himself on her, she slipped away and told the nuns.

She remembered the soothing music of the nuns she'd heard at the ruins and before on the first night at Cleaves, when she thought it must be coming from next door. From Lucille's.

Lucille was safe like the nuns. She *would* tell Lucille! She would go down the shaft and find her now. The garderobe might not be how the first Rosamund escaped, but it was ready for the second one!

She tiptoed up the tower steps, leaving the door only slightly ajar. She didn't switch on the light, although dusk gathered outside the deep windows.

Scratching came from across the room. Homer sounded as if he were giving his bedding a major turn-

102

out. His cage stood with its mesh door facing the wall, but far enough away to allow air circulation. Books were stacked on top and a heap of clothes dumped around.

Rosamund dragged the clobber out of the alcove. The bicycle torch and tie lay in the shadows against the wall.

She felt along the board and pulled out the cork plug. Then she scrabbled up the wood with her fingernails. She had lifted both boards clear and was winding the tie round her head when she heard Richard calling.

She went dead still, uncertain what to do. She could get into the shaft and pull the boards overhead, but what about Homer?

Richard would come up looking for her and hear him. He'd go berserk. He'd probably chuck him out of a tower window.

While she hesitated, she heard Richard's voice louder, calling from the bottom of the tower steps. She jammed the planks in place and pressed them even with her fist. Then she flung Sam's gear back into the alcove.

She tore across and opened the door.

'There you are!' boomed Richard rising round the curve. 'Catherine just phoned. I shouted, but you didn't answer.'

Why hadn't she realised Mum would ring! 'Has she gone now? Can I call her back?'

'Still interviewing. I told her Sam had deserted us and you must be buried in a book. We sounded jolly dull.'

'I was looking for something up here.'

Richard turned and Rosamund had no choice but to

follow him back down the spiral.

'I'm too tired to read anymore,' she said when they reached the bottom. 'I think I'll go to bed.'

She walked past him, trying to sound matter-of-fact. 'Goodnight. See you in the morning.'

He didn't answer.

She shut her door, then waited on the other side to hear him go away. Footsteps went back towards the tower. Had he heard Homer's scratching and decided to investigate? No, he went into the tower bathroom.

Now what? Wait and try again later. Keep her clothes on, but pretend she'd gone to bed.

After a bit, she heard Richard walk slowly along the passage. But there was no sound of clacking stairs. He must have gone into his bedroom.

She left her hair in plaits to keep it out of her eyes for climbing. She took off her trainers and got into bed with the lights off. Trembling, she pulled the duvet over her shorts and T-shirt.

The claw in her stomach gripped tighter.

A tense stillness filled the room. She lay with her eyes fixed on the door, waiting to see the crack of light from the passageway go off or hear Richard go downstairs. She watched and listened for ages.

Then the door moved. Richard's huge figure filled the doorway. She could see the dark shape of his dressing gown and bare feet against the light in the passage.

The door closed. Terrified, she saw him steal towards her.

104

Chapter 13

The air crackled. When Richard got near the bed, Rosamund snapped her eyes shut. Perhaps he'd go away if he thought she were asleep.

He lifted the duvet.

She pretended to wake up and be surprised. 'What's the matter?'

'Nothing, sweetie. I'm lonely, so I've come to see you.' He started to get in bed.

'Don't be silly. You can't get in here.'

'Be friendlier to me, Rosamund.'

'I'm asleep.'

'I'll cuddle you.'

'Please go away. I'll tell Mum.'

'She knows I wouldn't hurt you. I won't hurt you. Your imagination's been running away with you lately, hasn't it?' He pushed in beside her.

He'll lie to Mum, Rosamund thought helplessly. He won't say he got in bed.

'Just snuggle up,' Richard crooned. 'You like a cuddle, don't you?' He started kissing her face. 'You're so lovely.'

The air bit and spat chunks of electric static. They spun at Rosamund and made her fierce.

'Stop it!' she yelled. She jerked free. Screaming, she dived forwards and plunged down the bed.

Richard jumped up and cut off her way to the door. She backed into the corner of the panels as he came towards her.

'Go away!' she shouted. 'You've no right to touch me.'

'Don't act like this, Rosamund,' he coaxed. 'I love you. I really do. You'll see how nice I can be.' At the same time, he lifted his hands away from his sides ready to grab her if she bolted.

The air turned shrill, charging its currents into her body. '*No*!' it screeched. She let it through. '*No*! *No*! *No*!' she screamed.

'Shut up, you minx!' he ordered. 'I'm not hurting you. Get back in bed!' He tried to drag her out of the corner.

She pressed into the panels, hitting out to fend him off.

'Leave me alone!' she cried. He was too big, too strong to take on by herself.

He seized one of her plaits. 'Come here!'

The hair ripped from its fasteners. Pain shot through her head as he yanked.

'*Help*!' she wailed.

Suddenly, the panel behind her jumped and slid away. It sent her crashing sideways with Richard on top. They looked up into a shaft of light.

A woman stood there. White hair fell onto a long white gown.

Richard roared with terror and leaped back. Rosamund got to her knees and thrust her arms through

106

the gap. She clung to the shining woman, sobbing.

Then Richard realised that the wall had opened into another part of the house. The woman was Lucille.

He staggered to his feet. 'She's hysterical!' he shouted. 'I'll leave her to you!' He rushed out of the room.

Lucille helped Rosamund through the opening. She pressed catches and closed panels in Rosamund's room and on the minstrels' gallery.

She talked soothingly all the time. 'It's all right. You're safe, dear. Safe.'

'He got in bed!' sobbed Rosamund.

'You're with me now,' Lucille said tenderly. 'It's over.'

One arm cradling her, she led Rosamund along the gallery to her bedroom. She nestled a soft shawl around Rosamund's shoulders and then put a dressing gown over her long nightdress.

They went down to the little sitting room at the end of the screens passage.

Rosamund huddled against Lucille on the sofa. 'What if you hadn't got to me?' She cried her way through tissue after tissue from the box Lucille rested on the sofa arm. In between using the tissues, she held Lucille's hand.

'Those panels were how the first Rosamund escaped, weren't they? Then down and out through the screens passage and over the bridge.'

Lucille nodded. 'I think so. That's why I couldn't bring myself to mention them to the builder when the house was divided. They must have been put in when Rosamund's father made the new great hall.'

Rosamund stared at the raised veins and brown-mottled skin on the back of Lucille's hand. 'If this had been an ordinary house, I wouldn't have got away. I decided to come to you, but I'd left it too late.'

Lucille fetched some hot milk. They drank it in the china cups with flowers on.

The painful memories pushed out, starting with Victoria Road and the way Richard looked at her and touched her clothes there. She knew Lucille believed everything.

'It's very good you're telling me, dear. I'll help you,' she said. 'I'll ring next door and say you're staying tonight.'

'Thank you!'

'And Mum will be back tomorrow? Shall we talk to her together?'

Rosamund drew her knees onto the sofa and hugged them. 'I'll mess things up. She wants everything to be great with Richard.'

'You aren't to blame for what happened,' Lucille said firmly. 'You aren't to blame for any of it.'

Richard told Cathy on the phone that Rosamund had had another nightmare. He'd let Lucille look after her. No doubt she would be full of more absurd tales.

When Cathy knocked on Lucille's open door, Rosamund ran into her arms.

108

'Mum!' She held her tight and began to cry.

'Oh, darling! More bad dreams! Have you got a fever?'

'Welcome back, Cathy,' said Lucille. 'Come in, my dear.'

'Thank you for taking care of Ros.'

'Come down to the sitting room, dear,' Lucille said.

Mum gave her an anxious glance. 'What's the matter?'

They sat down. Lucille quietly folded her hands in her lap. 'We've got something very serious to talk about. It's going to be difficult for you to believe, Cathy dear, but we must make truth a friend.'

'Mum, Richard attacked me!' Rosamund burst out. 'He tried to be sexual!'

'What?' Mum frowned. 'Darling, you're imagining it. I'm sure he was only being affectionate. He certainly wasn't being sexual.'

'He *was*! He *was*!' sobbed Rosamund. 'It isn't the first time. I've been trying to tell you!'

Lucille told Mum what she'd heard and seen. Rosamund choked back her tears and described the whole of yesterday evening. Then the other times poured out, jumbled and confused, but told to Mum at last.

Mum looked wide-eyed from one of them to the other like a scared animal. Finally, she jumped up.

'I'm going to have this out with Richard!' She went next door to ring him in private.

Her eyes were bloodshot when she came back. 'He won't admit he meant anything wrong, but I know he's lying. I can hear it in his voice.'

She sat down and put her head in her hands. 'It's so hard to accept. *Oh, God, help us*!'

Lucille put her arms around her.

'What are we going to do?' Mum cried.

'Make sure it stops,' said Lucille. 'Perhaps you would like to talk to the people at social services? Sad to say, they're used to supporting families with this problem.'

Mum found the number. She clutched the receiver with both hands. Her knuckles went white.

'We've got an appointment for this afternoon,' she told Rosamund when she hung up.

They saw a social worker and a woman police officer. They asked Rosamund if a video recorder could run while they talked.

'It will save you having to repeat things,' said the social worker gently. 'Indecent assault is against the law. The video can be used as evidence.'

Rosamund started. Evidence! She looked to see whether Mum minded that Richard could be prosecuted.

'Although legal action may be taken, the most important thing is that Richard admit to himself the harm he's been causing,' the social worker said.

'Yes, he must,' Mum agreed woodenly.

'He can have therapy. He can also join a sex offenders' group. He'll hear how other people are working to recover.'

When they got back to the car, Mum sat staring through the windscreen.

Rosamund whispered, 'Perhaps we shouldn't have gone to social services.'

Mum turned at once. 'Yes we should! We all need help. What was I doing rushing us into a set-up with someone we only half knew? How appropriate, Sam naming him Sir Richard. That's just what I wanted him to be – a knight riding up to give us all a happy ending.'

She began to shake with sobs, heaving out her words. 'I wouldn't – listen – I wouldn't – see –'

'Oh, Mum! ' cried Rosamund wretchedly. 'I was so *frightened*!'

Mum held her. 'My precious! How could I have – left you unprotected?'

Tears spilled down their faces and onto their clothes. Mum tried to kiss Rosamund's away.

'I'm so – very – sorry!' Her voice ached with such pain that Rosamund had no doubt how truly she meant it. 'Oh, my darling – Forgive – me. *Please* forgive me!'

They clung to each other for a long time, grieving for what had happened, wishing it away, but knowing that it had to be part of them now.

The police charged Richard later that day. He got bail on condition that he moved out for the time being.

Although he wasn't around, Rosamund kept having panic attacks. Fear dug in her stomach as if she were about to be grabbed.

The worst attack happened not long before they left

111

Cleaves at the end of the summer. Sweating, she hunched on the bed, squeezing herself small. She wanted to run, but where could you run from terror that was inside?

'Help me,' she moaned.

Hugging herself, she limped over to Rosamund's picture.

Like a wind blast, fury overtook her. Richard's easel was holding Rosamund! She twisted the clamp screw and yanked the drawing board free. She ran with it to the bed, propping the picture against the panelling.

Then she squared up to the easel. It stood there smugly waiting to receive anything else she might paint. Well, it wasn't going to!

She kicked the easel's legs out from under it. After the crash, she kicked and stamped again and again so hard that it hurt through her trainers. Holding the wooden frame down with stinging feet, she wrenched a strut until it snapped. She hurled it down the room. She trampled and wrenched and broke until the easel was nothing but a heap of firewood.

She collapsed on the floor, weeping. She felt broken herself. Exhausted. Empty.

She looked at the first Rosamund's picture. Perhaps she had got her wrong after all. How could she be so full of life, flourishing, ready to spin off the paper laughing?

But even the brass memorial in the church had Rosamund smiling.

'How did you get from this to that?' she asked miserably.

The answer came deep inside. *Keep going! Look after yourself. Help will come.*

She and Mum and Sam were together. She was going to see a therapist. Julie would live nearby again when they moved. And she had Lucille.

She and Lucille were going to trim the herb hedges today. She got up and went to find her.

Going Forward

Rosamund and Sam left the bikes and ran through the enclosed garden. Rosamund noticed spring shoots on the Rosa mundi rose.

In Lucille's sitting room, the little table waited for them, laden with tea things. In the centre sat a round rich cake.

'The fruit cake looks great!' said Sam.

'Which one?' asked Lucille with an expression something like Sam's own grin.

Everyone's eyes travelled beyond the table to an oak chest where Lucille's decorated straw hat lay cheerfully waiting the return of summer. Lucille and Sam chuckled at each other.

'And how's Homer?' asked Lucille.

'Brilliant. He loves being a town mouse. Feels at *home* at last. I'd have brought him to see you, if we hadn't been on bikes.'

'You must take him some edible fruit cake with my best wishes.'

Mum usually brought and fetched Rosamund when she visited Lucille. They chose times Richard would be at work.

'Do you feel frightened having Richard next-door after you helped me?' Rosamund had asked Lucille.

'No, dear,' said Lucille. 'I believe the best part of him

114

is glad it stopped.'

Rosamund thought that might be true. She had started going to a group of girls who had all been molested. It helped to talk about her feelings where everyone understood.

And listening to the others, she began to realise that the people who hurt them weren't happy. She wondered if bad things happened to Richard when he was a boy.

While they were having second cups of tea, Lucille produced a big envelope. 'Look what I found when I was tidying a drawer.'

She pulled out a large photograph with curling edges. 'This was taken in the great hall in the nineteenth century. When the family still lived here. It was with the papers when my parents bought Cleaves.'

Rosamund studied the old photo. Furniture packed the hall, but behind it the painted cloth hung in the same place.

'Rosamund's story doesn't end in that hole!' she exclaimed.

The photo had the last scene. The first Rosamund stood in front of the manor. She held open her arms to welcome three nuns carrying bundles.

'Why are the nuns coming to Cleaves?'

'King Henry forced a lot of religious houses to close in 1536. Rosamund took in the nuns who had no families to care for them.'

'So she repaid them!'

'They lived here at Cleaves, and Rosamund and her husband shared their time between Cleaves and his manor.'

'And the nuns would have gone on singing their services here?'

Lucille smiled at Rosamund. 'They would.'

Smiling back into Lucille's face with its fragile skin and million creases, Rosamund suddenly saw her as an old woman who would be very old before long. A woman who might need her help.

I'll try to repay you too, she thought. I will always, always be your friend.

'Are we going to pick some blossom for you to sketch, dear?' asked Lucille.

'Yes, please.'

'I think I'll get my coat then.'

'Let me,' said Rosamund.

'Thank you. It's on the bed.'

'You had the way through the wall closed off, didn't you?'

'Yes, dear.'

'Mum made me nail up the garderobe too,' said Sam.

Rosamund hadn't been upstairs since they left Cleaves. Lucille had taught her to take deep slow breaths whenever she started to feel panicky. *In, out, in, out,* she breathed as she climbed to the minstrels' gallery.

She walked a little way along the gallery and leaned her cheek against the panelling. She imagined the room on the other side – the sun streaming through the big arched window, the coloured lights.

116

Was the first Rosamund there? It didn't matter really. She had Rosamund's story inside her.

'Thank you,' she whispered. 'I think I'm going to be okay now.'

Did she? Yes, she did feel a breeze. And there was a gentle sigh.